SYBIL NORCROFT BOOK ELEVEN

PRESIDENT
SYBIL NORCROFT

Rumors of War, Secession, and Trouble

BY
CARL DOUGLASS

Neurosurgeon turned Author writes with
Gripping Realism

We Believe In The Power Of Authors

PO Box 221974 Anchorage, Alaska 99522-1974
books@publicationconsultants.com—www.publicationconsultants.com

ISBN Number: 978-1-63747-075-6
eBook ISBN Number: 978-1-63747-076-3

Library of Congress Number: 2022936380

Copyright 2022 Carl Douglass
—First Edition—

All rights reserved, including the right of
reproduction in any form, or by any mechanical
or electronic means including photocopying or
recording, or by any information storage or
retrieval system, in whole or in part in any
form, and in any case not without the
written permission of the author and publisher.

Manufactured in the United States of America

CHAPTER ONE

As the presidency of Sybil Norcroft Daniels entered its fourth year—the second year of her having been elected president—each of her ongoing struggles grew worse, even as she became more facile at her job. She continued to have to do patchwork fixes of the continually growing secession problem. Iran's new president, Naveed Ali Mazanderani, was even more intransigent and bellicose than his predecessor. Mazanderani was well known as an Islamist—of the Shia stripe–but just as much an extremist as the new leaders of the Islamic State organization in Syria. He openly boasted of having ICBMs with nuclear warheads of Iranian design and manufacture.

His common threat besides "Death to the Great Satan" was that his missile forces were ready at any time to launch the "End of Days Weapon" if America did not remove its sanctions. And—as if to make President Daniels a believer in eternal life–the dictator of North Korea had "miraculously been resurrected from the dead" and the generals who had the audacity to suggest that they should succeed him had mysteriously dropped out of mention in public. Kim Jong Un and his sister Kim Yo-jong appeared to maintain their stranglehold on the DPRK with even more than their former excessive power. Kim was beginning to make threatening statements against the United States again.

In her State of the Union in the first week of February, Sybil mainly touted her successes in dealing with the insurrection, the reconstruction, repair, and maintenance of the nation's infrastructure, and the reaffirmation of US/UK friendship and partnership. It made her a little displeased with herself that she had not had much to say about the real problems looming over her administration and the citizens of America.

She muttered inwardly fairly often that she was becoming as much of a double-talking president as her predecessors. It was her basic personality to present and to defend the truth and her authentic self. But she had learned the hard lesson that almost all politicians learn as they move into the passing years in office: you have to go along to get along. You may enter the political arena with refreshing candor and idealism; but you soon learn that you follow the political party's lead; or you get nowhere. She had lately been finding herself answering reporters' honest questions with non-sequiturs and sometimes outright lies to save herself personal embarrassment or to protect friends from embarrassment or worse—malfeasance or even outright criminality.

She had early on become aware that the chances of her historical legacy being that of a stateswoman were slipping away, and she was lowering her own bar by countenancing "white lies"–a phrase she despised–and using euphemisms when the truth was less than flattering to her.

"*Heavy sigh,*" Sybil said to herself every time one of her arch enemies spoke in public.

It was in that frame of mind that President Daniels learned of a scheme that had been going on since she was inaugurated, that was likely to become her "Teapot Dome Scandal", the one that had hounded President Warren G. Harding to the end of his presidency and hastened his death. A whistle blower informant acting from within the Department of the Interior came forward with a declaration of malfeasance in office of the departmental secretary, undersecretary, three Interior attorneys, and a consortium of ten major developer cronies who were serious donors to both political parties and who were considered "too big to fall".

President Daniels did not know who the whistle blower was, but she was informed–in no uncertain terms–by the inspector general of the Department of the Interior and by her attorney general that the facts were essentially irrefutable and backed by a wealth of objective evidence secreted out of the department's files and by hacking into the secretary's personal e-mails and those of the developer/donors.

She was caught between a rock and a hard place. If she came down hard on the miscreants, she would surely lose them as donors and would gain the lasting enmity of the politicians who were the recipients. Not a few of those politicians also stood to gain major financial windfalls from their investments in the schemes. If she allowed or encouraged the truth to come out in all its ugly glory, she would spare herself criticism; but the scandal would forever taint her political legacy, even though she herself would be legally established as having had no foreknowledge or direct or even indirect involvement in the schemes. She could not be implicated as having profited from the venture; she had not even received political donations from anyone involved... thankfully.

When she was fully informed of the criminality and venality of what became known as the "Other Teapot Tempest", Sybil privately moaned to herself, quoting the Master of the House from *Les Miserable*, "*What to do? What to do? What's a poor Christian to do?*"

Simply put, the scandal was this: Congress passed a bill allowing for the drilling of undersea oil reserves off the coasts Hawaii and Florida providing loans totaling $989, 376, 000. The government's purpose was to ensure that the national petroleum repository was filled to the brim to ensure against future OPEC economic attacks and to keep US petroleum businesses healthy. The law was complicated and lengthy, but it forbad the sale of rights to any company or individual lacking a bond guaranteeing full payment to the government if the business venture failed to progress or to repay speculators for their full investments. That particular clause was placed because of several speculative offshore offerings that used government money as startup loans and to offset initial production costs.

For a variety of reasons, every one of the ventures permitted and financed by the US government failed; the principles defaulted and filed bankruptcy. As a result, innocent private investors and the trusting government were left holding the worthless paper while the speculators—most of whom oversold their capabilities—had absconded or filed bankruptcy. Some committed outright fraud, counting on obtaining government money, never making even a pretense of beginning work, and walked away with the money and intentionally left the government to deal with the unconscionable consequences.

In addition, other clauses expressly forbad drilling in certain fragile areas or where local governments had established prohibitive laws. Most of the perpetrators simply ignored that requirement, just as had been the practice in the past in an industry rife with wild cowboys and charlatans.

In this "Other Teapot Tempest", government auditors and FBI investigators were able to make viable legal cases and were proceeding towards arrests and arraignments. Examples of the fraudulent actions included: offshore drilling contractor Excelsior Corporation which obtained federal funds to be able to guarantee that there would be sufficient money for the actual building and drilling contractors to proceed. A month later, Excelsior withdrew, citing the recent sharp decline of oil price due to the oil oversupply and drop in demand caused by COVID-19, as the reason.

The federal investigators found a pile of paperwork in neat folders in the company's office—none of which was a true account of risk, loss, or profit. Worse, there was no record of loan payments. The principles of the company were nowhere to be found; their names, addresses, telephone numbers, and e-mail addresses, were all phonies. The only genuine document in the pile was the filing for bankruptcy, except that the spaces for the names of the officers of the corporation were left blank.

A genuine provider of drilling services to oil and gas companies, Rand-Carter Ltd, announced after Excelsior's disappearance that it had analyzed its situation of falling oil prices and concluded that oil prices and the Covid-19 effect on economies would negatively affect its business and results gravely in the sort-run.

Rand-Carter applied for Chapter 11 bankruptcy as the result of the downturn and the profound uncertainty surrounding the degree and duration of the disruptions, and the general inability to predict with any reasonable accuracy the magnitude, pace, or duration, of any recovery. The company officers worked with the investigators and agreed to testify against the Excelsior Corporation. The government agreed to allow Rand-Carter additional time to put its affairs in order in the hope that conditions would improve enough to make drilling once again profitable. No one said anything about the small investors, many of whom had lost all their savings.

Several cabinet departments became involved and worked to persuade OPEC to raise its prices across the board by 2022. Saudi Arabia, Russia, and the United

States, signed the agreement, but made it contingent upon Mexico and South America signing the agreement. Therein lay another egregious layer of fraud.

Additional investigation by OPEC's fraud division in conjunction with the FBI turned up a company previously unknown to the American and Saudi petroleum contracting world. The company—which had been in existence on paper for just short of a year—was called AmiAramco Petroleum Ltd to take advantage of the similarity in naming to Saudi Arabia's national oil company Saudi Aramco. The company received $100 million from the US government as start-up money for its drilling joint venture. Their plans included commencement of drilling in the UK's southern North Sea, in the Guyana-Suriname basin, and in the *Vaca Muerta's* vast resources, despite the political situation in Argentina being uncertain, to put the problems in the least troublesome light.

Another company—a real company—named Cherokee Drilling already announced a major discovery, drilled a test well, and had successfully created a geyser. Their problem was that the oil was found below 20,000 feet and was seriously over-pressured making retrieval difficult and dangerous. Cherokee was waiting for American and Argentine investigators to determine if the risks of a disastrous oil spill were less than the fabulous profits to be made. AmiAramco Petroleum successfully solicited private investment funds without reporting the serious limitations of their proposed project.

Another fraud ridden on-paper company—Petro-Brazil—inveigled investors–including the US government–

to the tune of $90 million to begin drilling in the same lower Santonian level and in addition for drilling in the Santos Basin of Brazil, and the Tumbes Basin of Peru. The principles were in the wind by the time President Sybil Daniels learned about their colossal fraud.

Legitimately, the Bahamas Petroleum Company announced plans to start drilling 200 miles off the coast of southern Florida but had not yet been given the green light by the US or the State of Florida. Their documentation and exploration evidence appeared to be in order, and permission was expected to be granted. However, a second company—again one unfamiliar to the usual petroleum contractors—named Bah-Flor Drilling, had successfully used insider information and employed corrupt Florida state senators to get a speedy okay.

Later–when the legal dust settled down–it was proved that Bah-Flor Drilling had simply purloined the materials submitted by Bahamas Petroleum Company to get past the legitimate evaluators. Bahamas Petroleum's progress was severely impaired after Hurricane Esmerelda ravaged the islands and caused a major oil spill on Grand Bahama island. It was in dire need of a successful venture off Florida to recoup, but now that seemed an unlikely prospect— another casualty of Mother Nature and fraudsters.

Bah-Flor Drilling had somehow neglected to mention that small impediment to obtaining permission to drill. In addition to stealing the government funds, the principles also made off with $20 million of private investment funds, which were laundered through Grand Cayman banks. The money and the thieves were long gone and lost to history.

An altogether bona vide company–NemoDeep Petroleum Drilling Consortium–had the misfortune to lose its five drilling platforms to a later hurricane, and Mexico and the world suffered from a spill of 229 million gallons of crude into the Gulf of Mexico. Pet-AmiMex Drilling was not deterred by the fact that the oil spill stopped all drilling in the Gulf, killed the Mexico/American deep drilling ventures, and caused the Bahamas to prevent all drilling in Bahamian waters for the foreseeable future.

The scrappy Pet-AmiMex Drilling company ignored all that, convinced the US Dept. of Commerce officials linked to what became Daniels' "Other Teapot Tempest", to allow $86 million dollars of American tax payer money to be used for their drilling scam. The principles in that fraud outdid P.T. Barnum and rivaled Elizabeth Holmes, Charles Ponzi, and Bernie Madoff, by hoodwinking well-heeled private investors out of another $100 million to bring in billions of dollars-worth of oil. The oil was real; but the drilling prospectus was not; and the real money went into the same section of the ether as had the Pet-AmiMex Drilling funds. Someone, somewhere, was enjoying mint juleps sitting on the veranda of an idyllic Caribbean island mansion.

Because of OPEC's internal bi-national competition between Russia and Saudi Arabia, the "Other Teapot Tempest", the steep decline in petroleum usage due to the global requirements for people to quarantine at home because of COVID-19 fears, and because no one could trust anyone in the business for the time being, Mexico closed off its waters to drilling and prevented its own contractors from doing business of drilling or doing any business with foreigners. For the odd reason that the most powerful person in the world must somehow be responsible, President Daniels began to get the blame in the world's press. South America followed Mexico's lead and closed off its waters. Valenzuela with its failing economy and history of hatred of America since the Hugo Chavez administration jumped on the anti-Daniels bandwagon with a little help from China and Russia.

As the deluge of bad press continued to rain down on the president, *The Enquirer* dropped a bomb. All Sybil's enemies calculated that it would be or at least fervently hoped that it would be the last piece of artillery needed to cause her administration to collapse.

A front-page photo purported to be Sybil. The beautiful blond was in the buff and was about to take a cocktail from a very handsome, strikingly well-muscled, young man with long curly blond hair. He was wearing a speedo, that scarcely covered the essentials. The blond—looking for all the world to be a dead ringer for the sitting president of the United States–was wearing a languid, satisfied smile. The triple-sized headline in all caps read, PRETTY PRESIDENT PREFERS BOY TOY TO HUBBY. Below the huge photo was a quote attributed to Marilyn Monroe after her famous risqué calendar became public.

"A pompous visitor asked ~~Marilyn Monroe~~ (Sybil Daniels) at Niagara: 'Is it true that when you posed for that famous photograph, ~~Miss Monroe~~, (Missy President) you had nothing on?" 'No," said ~~Marilyn~~, (Sybil) 'I had the radio on.'"

In the White House residence, Sybil showed Charles the copy of the *Enquirer* given to her by her secretary, Mrs. Carpentier.

He looked at it and laughed, "Well, Sybil, nice pic, but it looks like your head is on sideways."

CHAPTER TWO

With encouragement from her ever-safeguarding husband, Sybil set out to meet each of the challenges of the past week, the last one first. She was embarrassed and wanted to hide because of the weeklong barrage from the tabloids about her supposed illegitimate island lover. The *Enquirer* ran the photo in another issue using a deep pink filter, thereby spuriously increasing the heat. The headline for that photo was: "PRESIDENT SYBIL DANIELS IN LOVE TRYST WITH HANDSOME MYSTERY MAN". The photo and the suggestion of infidelity on her part irritated her greatly; she was better known for being rather puritanical; and this onslaught called wrongful attention to her, indicating that she was a hypocrite as well as an adulteress. There is something worse than "Hell hath no fury, like a woman scorned." For Sybil, it read, "Hell hath no fury like a woman defamed!"

She very seldom utilized the services of a government agency for her personal purposes. However, her fury this time drove her to ask one from DCIA Martin Obershauer.

"Martin," she said as jauntily as she could muster, "I am calling to give you a little official titillation. I presume you have seen the last two issues of the Inquirer?"

"I have to confess that I did. Don't believe a word, and you and I both know that seeing is not believing."

"Thank you, My Friend. I need proof that the photo and the narratives are both false."

"Sounds like the brewing of a libel suit. I will get right on it. I think we will have the evidence before the end of the day. We will have the evidence packaged; so, it will be airtight. How's it gonna feel to become the owner of the *Enquirer*?"

"Even the thought of that makes me ill, Martin. I do appreciate your help and consider that I owe you one."

"I think we're pretty much even, Madam President. Take a rest from this and leave it to me."

Sybil told Charles what she was doing and asked him not to pursue it. She and Martin would take care of it on the down-low and without publicity. Satisfied that he was all right with her plan, Sybil dove into the next problem on the list—for some odd reason, going from the last to the first. She pondered the problem of the "Daniels' Other Teapot Tempest". She studied how President Warren G. Harding handled the original "Tea Pot Dome Scandal" and decided that none of what he did warranted a second thought. After all, the result of his efforts led directly to his death. She read a history of how Richard M. Nixon handled the Watergate Affair and decided that it was a thorough study in what not to do. She read transcripts of Bill Clinton's impeachment proceedings and marveled at his efforts at obfuscation. He had been saved by partisan politics in the same way one of his successors, Donald Trump had been. She called her presidential and White House attorneys and a defense attorney of her own—Roderick Michaelson—to attend an Oval Office strategy session.

"Gentlemen," Sybil said from behind the Resolute Desk, "I want you to work with Mr. Roderick Michaelson. There is a good deal of gossipy accusing going on in the press and to some degree in Congress more than suggesting that I knew about or aided and abetted in the criminal enterprise now being called 'the Other Teapot Tempest'. There are questions about what I knew, when I knew it, did I make money from it, and, if so, how much?"

Michaelson introduced himself to the White House attorney Lincoln Jukes and, the presidential attorney Carter Anderton.

"The president hired me to get ahead of these accusations, more than to defend her. I am convinced she had nothing to do with the crimes—note that I used the plural—and to put as much distance between her and the criminals as possible. I would appreciate it if you could make use of your resources to find out any connection…any whatever…President Daniels has had with any of them. Most of them who are still around will probably be deposed by federal and state lawyers, and I don't think we need to repeat those depositions.

However, I do think it is critical for us to depose Sam Nichols ASAP before anyone else gets to him. He is still occupying his position as secretary of the interior, and we need to know what evidence is available against him. I'll deal with that. I know it's a stretch, but we need to get our evidence together inside a week; so, President Daniels can look it over before she has her woodshed visit with Secretary Nichols. Remember, 'mum's' the word."

"Are we to understand that you are taking the lead?" Jukes asked and looked pointedly at the president.

"Yes. I don't want to step on any toes but working from the outside gives me some latitude you don't have or probably shouldn't exercise."

Jukes and Anderton nodded their agreement.

"So, then, Gentlemen, we best get to work."

Sybil thanked all three men and got back to her job of being president.

Michaelson persuaded Attorney General Philip Cragen to arrange a secret meeting with the 'Other Teapot Tempest' whistle blower, the Director of the FBI, and the Chairperson of the Senate Judiciary Committee to learn everything the whistle blower knew and to have every involved official privy to the same information at the same time.

Cragen laid down some rules: "This is top secret, and I am the only one cleared to deal with the whistle blower himself. Frankly, that is for reasons of national security, but more for the blower's personal security. We will all get to question the blower, but the deponent will be in another room using a telephonic voice disguiser. Your names will be part of the record, but the blower's will not be known to any of you. I will start the questioning and will decide about immunity and whistle blower rewards as soon as I'm convinced that the blower is the real thing and is entitled."

A telephone beeped on Cragen's desk.

He pushed a button and said, "This is Attorney General Philip Cragen. I will refer to you as 'blower' if that is all right to protect your anonymity. Is your attorney present?"

"Yes, Sir, came a Donald Duck voice.

It was difficult to be able to suppress a laugh.

"Am I talking to blower's attorney."

"Yes. And in the interest of my client's safety, I will remain anonymous as well."

"That's fine. We are using a one-way television communicator. You can see us, but we can't see you. You know that your audibles to us are disguised, but you will hear our actual voices."

"Agreed."

"Now then, Mr. Blower, your name and pertinent identifying information will be kept by your attorney until it comes time for you to testify in court or in Congress. Because of the nature of the crimes involved, you and your family will have around the clock security. The guards are experts, highly experienced; and I am sure you will never be aware of them. Do you agree with those arrangements, Sir?"

"I do," came the voice of Mickey Mouse.

Michaelson had to hold his hand over his mouth to keep from laughing out loud. It was bizarre.

"Please tell me and these lawyers how you came to obtain the information you are going to testify about today."

Blower readily admitted getting into restricted files of the Department of the Interior and of the department secretary. He began to admit hacking, when the attorney interrupted in his Donald Duck voice.

"We cannot proceed without a guarantee of immunity under the Whisteblower Protection Act of 1989, Mr. Cragen. It is possible that some of the information came as a result of what could be possibly be interpreted as criminal acts. As you know, whistleblowers take a very real risk of facing reprisal and retaliation from those who are accused or alleged of wrongdoing. Anonymity is imperative as well as immunity."

"Probably," the attorney general said quietly, "but we came here for the truth, and have no reason at this point to believe that Blower is the real culprit in this matter. Therefore, so long as you tell us the full and unvarnished truth, you have official immunity granted by me. Any crimes we happen to find after this deposition to which you have not admitted to us, may be subject to criminal investigation. Do we have an understanding?"

"We do," Mickey Mouse said.

Donald Duck told Mickey to continue.

Blower explained in detail how he or she hacked into the department's and Secretary Caspar's computers and into those of several of the individuals involved in the scandal. He admitted to going through restricted files of other officers and employees of the Interior Department and to making copies of documents that pertained to the criminal enterprise. Blower took an hour and forty-five minutes to give an accountant's level of precise presentation of the evidence.

When the Blower finished, Cragan asked for an estimate of how much money changed hands and came into the possession of Secretary Caspar.

Mickey answered without hesitation, obviously reading from documents or notes, "$14,674,000."

"Do you have documentation of that amount of malfeasance, Sir?"

"I do. The evidence is in the hands of my attorney and will be ready when needed."

"Then, Sir, if all this pans out, you will receive at least thirty percent of what the government collects. You should be a very wealthy person when the dust finally settles."

Mickey giggled.

"The other attorneys have some more questions of their own, Mr. Blower. Are you okay to continue?"

"I am."

"Hello, Mr. Blower. My name is Roderick Michaelson. I am the personal attorney of President Sybil Norcroft Daniels, and I will probably only have a few questions for you."

"Fine," Mickey said.

"Sir, do you know the president personally?"

"No. I have never met her."

"Ever talked to her on the phone? Sent or received an e-mail between you and the president? Done business together? Been given a direct order from her?"

"No, no, no, and no. I hope that I enough 'no's," Mickey said.

"I know that was a compound question, but you did very well. So far as you know or can recollect, have you or anyone in your family ever had anything to do with the president or her family or staff on a social or personal basis?"

"None."

"Did President Daniels ever ask you to funnel money to her?"

"No."

"In your research or in any communications you recorded or witnessed, did you ever become aware that President Daniels ever participated in any way in the criminal actions undertaken by the individuals of whom you are aware?"

"Never."

"Remember, Mr. Blower, you are under oath a federal government legal proceeding. Do you wish to add, subtract, or to change any of the testimony you have given today?"

"Absolutely not." Mickey was adamant.

The other attorneys decided that they had all the information they needed and said they had no questions.

Secretary of the Interior Sam Nichols was holed up in his palatial ranch house on his property in Laramie, Wyoming, dreading the day when he would inevitably have to face the Snow Queen president back in DC.

A robust knock came on the door. It could not be anything good, thought Sam. Nobody ever comes way out here, and nobody knows I'm here.

He walked as slowly as possible to the front door and peered through the peep hole. He saw two men, one in the uniform of a US Marshal and the other a man in a charcoal grey suit and power tie—obviously an attorney.

He manufactured a smile and welcomed the gentlemen in.

"Long trip for you," he said, "can I offer you a libation?"

"No thanks," the man in the suit said. "Are you Sam Nichols, Secretary of the Interior for the United States government?"

"Yes. What's this all about?"

He knew it was lame, but he should be excused because he was hungover.

The marshal said, "Mr. Secretary, we need you to come with us."

"Where?"

"Washington DC. We have a warrant for your arrest. You can come with us voluntarily and without an attorney, and we do not need to serve the warrant at this point. Or, you can summon your attorney to meet us in Washington, and we can serve the warrant. Your choice."

"Do I need to be handcuffed?"

"Do you?" the marshal asked pointedly.

"I will cooperate."

The marshal service jet whisked the three men to Andrews Air Force Base. A jet-black SUV was waiting for them on the tarmac.

"This way, Mr. Secretary," the driver directed.

The four drove to the north entrance of the White House; and the marshal, the attorney, and the person of interest, were escorted without ceremony to the Oval Office.

President Daniels sat behind her desk and did not get up to greet the secretary. Nichols took that to be an ill-harbinger of things to come.

He was right. The president asked the marshal to remain as a witness, and for Roderick Michaelson to be available for additional questions if necessary.

"We will have some questions for you, Mr. Nichols. However, we are waiting for your attorney to arrive. She as promised to be no more than ten more minutes from now. We can sit and relax while we wait."

Sybil had been around the block before as an interrogator. The wait, she knew would serve to unnerve her quarry.

Five minutes later, Mrs. Carpentier knocked softly and entered with a sturdy looking middle-aged woman wearing her class A attorney uniform—navy blue suit, flat-soled black orthopedic shoes, and a white shirt. Her only adornment was a lanyard holding her White House pass.

"Gwendolyn Gertsch," I presume," said the president.

"Yes, Madam President. I am here to represent my client, Sam Nichols."

"Good, then we can begin."

Sybil was holding a thick blue folder full of the information faxed from the Laramie marshal's office. Sybil made a point of holding it in plain view.

CHAPTER THREE

President Sybil Norcroft Daniels had practiced improving her innate icy stare throughout her life—grade school, high school, university, medical school, PhD program, neurosurgery residency, as an internationally famous medical consultant for a TV network, as a CIA agent and as the DCIA, as the VP, and for four years of her presidency. She had it down pat, and it was altogether genuine.

She let Secretary Nichols stew in his own juices for a couple of minutes before speaking. She decided to come down hard.

"Have we ever met, ever talked, ever shared e-mails, texts, instagrams, tweets, Facebook, or telephone conversations, Sam?"

"Not that I'm aware of."

"Did you and I ever do any form of business with each other whatsoever?"

"No, Ma'am."

"So, you are on your own in this ongoing criminal conspiracy I'm reading about in the news?"

Ms Gertsch turned to her client, and he got the drift without her having to speak.

"On advice of my attorney, Madam President, I respectfully decline to answer your questions under my rights under the Fifth Amendment to the Constitution because to do so might cause me to incriminate myself."

"You're taking the coward's way out, taking the Fifth, are you Sam?"

"I respectfully decline to answer, and I cannot be nor shall be compelled in any criminal case to be a witness against myself, Ma'am."

"I think we're done here, Madam President," Ms. Gertsch said and stood up.

"I think you are almost right, Ms. Gertsch. Except for one thing."

She turned her glacial gaze at Sam Nichols again and said quietly with icicles hanging on every word, "Sam Nichols, you are fired. Federal officers will escort you out of this building and be present when you are once again granted access to your Interior office. That will be some time from now."

She looked away to her desk full of papers, and he and his attorney went away.

Sybil pressed a yellow button on her desk and summoned her appointments secretary.

"Did you get all that, Mrs. Carpentier?"

"Loud and clear. No problem with any lawyers or lawmakers hearing what the man had to say. I distinctly heard the phrase... the Fifth... more than once."

She smiled.

Sybil called the secretary of the Treasury with one question:

"Is it possible, permissible, or advisable, to withdraw treasury funds to shore up the companies innocently caught up in this so-called "Other Tea Pot Scandal"?

"Madam President, as I understand the law it is possible and permissible under the emergency circumstances we outlined before. This is a very flimsy reason, something like the great bank bailout some years ago. The circumstances in that incident were far more tenable than in this one. Is it advisable? Definitely not. Any bailout would seem to your enemies in Congress and throughout the American public as an oblique admission of guilt. Besides, these people all knew what they were risking. Oil speculation is easily the most dangerous investment there is, comparable to Monty Hall Three Door problem."

Sybil's eyebrows formed unspoken question marks.

"Your silence suggests that I have been a bit arcane for you. This is the gist of it: You're on a game show. The host offers you a choice among three doors. You know going in that behind one door is a new car; but behind the other two doors are prizes worth less than dollar. Behind the two doors are the cheesy cheap items. You pick door number 1. The audience takes note. The host—who is fully aware of what lies behind all the doors–then opens different door, not number 1; let's say number 3, this time. Oh, drat, you find nothing but a plastic doll. The host then makes his final offer: 'You can switch to door number 2 if you want.' Do you want to pick door number 2? So, Madam President, is it to your advantage to switch from your original choice?"

"I get it; I'm between a rock and a hard place for all of my apparent power."

"You are a quick learner, Madam President. Good for you."

The two friends laughed, and Sybil made a firm decision to do nothing and to let the scandal proceed forward under its own steam with her well out of it.

There is a good rule that states that when your desk is full of difficult problems, you should deal with most difficult one first. Sybil had been ridiculous in that regard. She had not named a vice-presidential candidate. She knew who it should be. He had been thoroughly vetted and was found to be a man without a flaw. In and of itself, that should be a reason not to make him her choice; but she knew that was irrational. She liked the man, and he had come around to agreeing to accept the nomination. Sybil could no longer hang fire. She called the office of the Senate Majority Leader Ralph Henry Nichols.

"Ralph, I know I have been putting you off, and I apologize. I am calling to ask you to accept Senator Franklin H. Tatum of California as my vice-presidential nominee."

"California doesn't seem like it would help your next re-election, Sybil. You sure about this?"

"I finely am, Ralph. Actually, I think California is at least as good as anyplace else, maybe better. All the people out west—what they call the flyover states—feel neglected because their people never seem to get anywhere. The Yalies and Harvard grads tend to corner the market. Besides, Franklin is a good man. He would make a good president—I think you would agree—in case of my death or incapacitation."

"Perish forbid. I guess he is as good as any and better than some. I'll get right on it."

"Thanks. I'll get back you on the petroleum bill. We need to do something, but I don't quite know what."

Acting under orders from the Kind Leader Kim Jong Un, the Strategic Rocket Forces of the DPRK fired a large ICBM into the ocean off the west coast of Hokkaido, Japan causing consternation in most of East Asia and in the United States. The ODNI informed President Daniels of the launch and told her that it seemed to have been successful, i.e. it landed where the North Koreans wanted it to. Two hours later Chairman Kim gave his usual gloating self-congratulatory speech and added that "our fears of the bullying Americans are now part of our past."

President Daniels convened the nation's security forces leaders to a round table discussion in the Situation Room.

"Kim is back to firing rockets again. Is this another phony political stunt, or should we worry about it?"

The DNI responded, "Madam President, there is something different this time. The rocket was larger, flew more accurately, and created a bigger ocean explosion.

They have improved. How many they have and how far they can go is a question for the MDA [Missile Defense Agency]."

"It is a true ICBM. We are not quite certain if it can hit the continental US, but it could easily take out Alaska or Hawaii. Our humint operatives assure us that they have stockpiled at least twenty of the missiles in the last two and a half years. We can no longer write them off as wannabees. They are unwelcome, but factual members of the club."

"Thank you. I'll open the discussion to everyone here. I want the best answer you've got about what we should do next," President Daniels said.

There was a wide range of suggestions which formed a continuum from more attempts at diplomacy; to give a little to get them to cease and desist, such as to lower the sanctions; to flyovers with B2 Stealth Bombers; to firing a shot across the bow (not precisely defined); and war (the type and degree of war not precisely defined).

Sybil gave them free reign to talk themselves out. When the responses began to grow less frequent and less vociferous, she signaled that she once again wanted to speak.

"An interesting discussion. There were suggestions from all over the map. Let me remind you that the US has tried diplomacy for thirty years, has raised and lowered sanctions, tried bribery, and has matched belligerence to belligerence, but never more.

"I hardly need to repeat my personal mantra. As president, I am not willing to send American boys and girls to die in a God-forsaken wicked little country in a regular land war where they are willing to suffer ten times the casualties that we do and consider that they have succeeded because we sue for peace. How well I remember what went on in Viet Nam when we won that war then gave them a full victory and bragging rights because our namby-pamby lefties corrupted our news outlets and our youth until we outright lost the war. 58,000 dead, and for what?

"We slinked out of Afghanistan with our tails between our legs, gave up the prisoners we were holding and countenanced the formation of the Taliban as a political entity that we formally recognized, after more than twenty years of fighting, with 2,400 American service members killed and 20,000 wounded in hostile action in that miserable low status backwater country. We got nothing but out of there."

She then spoke quietly, deliberately, and with absolute determination, "Enough awreddy. I refuse during my term or terms as president to allow even one more than absolutely necessary of our fine service members to 'pay the ultimate price' for another nonvictory. Up front, I will order a nuclear attack as my choice of 'shots across the bow'."

No one could fault her logic nor doubt her determination. This was a new kind of president; and the people in the Situation Room, and in the country, and throughout the world, were going to have to get used to a different kind of America.

Just before leaving the office to go to the residence to have a shower and to get dressed for another diplomatic dinner she detested, Sybil got a call from the DCIA Martin Obershauer.

"This is a secure line," Sybil said.

"I am also on a secure line, Madam President. This is for your eyes and ears only, as you requested. I am sending you a revised photograph of the *Enquirer's* front page of recent interest. Our shop has done a real day's work for you. First, the photo was obviously photo-shopped with your head put on a hootchy-kootchy dancer's body…quite poorly I might add. Your head was from a much younger picture of yours when your hair style was very different. Your head was canted at a very poor angle that made it look as if you turned you head quickly it would fall off. Our photo people were able to identify an unmistakable line of separation between the head and neck, clear evidence that it is a phony.

The body is that of Madonna Chambers, aka the "Boston Bombshell with the Best". Her part of the photoshopping was taken over fifteen years ago and is quite a bit less well defined compared to your more recent one—another clear indicator that the whole set-up is phony. We compared bikini shots of both of you from the past and more recently. Her recent photo shows her to be far less attractive, now with sooper-droopers and two chins. Your photo from your last family vacay in Newport Beach shows that you still rate a wolf whistle for your well-turned ankles."

They both laughed.

"You've made my day. We had a middle-aged trucker as a family friend who used to give a wolf-whistles to bedraggled mothers of three children pushing perambulators along the side walks as the truck drove past. Made the girl's day."

"The guy took a little more digging. We finally proved that he was photo-shopped to appear to be standing beside you. He is one Sergei Estronicov originally from Yekaterinburg, lately from Moscow Oblast. He has a record for prostitution, lewd behavior, and minor sexual assault. He is a handsome Viking looking lad with blond hair and a gym created slender build. He has worked mostly as a male model and apparently has helped several older women to be blackmailed by his work in the photoshopping scam business. We have alerted the Moscow Municipal Police. Apparently, they don't approve of such people or careers.

"We have made up an evidence package of the photoshopping. I personally think it's criminal, but it is at least a sure-thing for a civil defamation suit."

"Great work, Martin. I owe you."

"Oh, I'll hold you to that come budget time."

CHAPTER FOUR

Sybil mused to herself, "*Secession, what an ugly word,*" when the subject showed its ugly visage in late August. SCOTUS agreed to hear the motions for secession by fifteen different groups; but conspicuous by its absence from that list, was the CSA [Confederate States of America] because of its militant organization–the New Confederate Army–and its record of violence.

The New Confederate Army staged marches in the capitals throughout the states of the old confederacy: Montgomery, Alabama; Little Rock, Arkansas; Nashville, Tennessee; Jackson, Mississippi; Tallassee, Florida; Atlanta, Georgia; Austin, Texas; Raleigh, North Carolina; Columbia, South Carolina; Baton Rouge, Louisiana; and Richmond, Virginia. The marches were well organized and took place every other day—except Sunday—for three weeks, making local and national news headlines every day. The marchers were in neat, clean, Confederate army uniforms with spit and polish boots. They carried

AR-16s instead of Kentucky long rifles. In every city, the CSA spokespersons rented spaces along the parade routes and blasted their message of secession as loudly—and as often—as the law would allow. The first foray into national politics was peaceful and polite.

Sybil's Chief of Staff Gen. Omar Zabriskim, FBI Director Landon Murphy, and Attorney General Philip Cragen, met with President Daniels in the Oval Office at her request.

"Shades of Abraham Lincoln, but I have to ask: what should we do about the Confederate States of America and its would-be army?"

"Unlike in times past, the 'army' has done nothing overtly illegal, and every one of the marches went off by the book—legal in every state and city. As I see it, there is nothing we can do until they break the law," Attorney General Cragen said.

"And—much as I despise their point of view—they have the right to voice it; there is that little thing called the First Amendment to the Constitution," added DFBI Murphy.

"You know perfectly well that they plan violence if SCOTUS does not hear their case," the President said. "Are they being surveilled?"

"SCOTUS is not going to go through the agony of secession again, certainly not for a wanna be new Confederate States of America. So... I suppose we are going to cope with more violence. And, yes, they are under close—but very careful—scrutiny. It won't go well if our agents are caught."

"Did the CSA or its New Confederate Army participate against the government during the recent bloody and destructive insurgency?" asked President Daniels.

"I have a complicated and silly set of answers; yes, to the first, and no, to us being able to prove it. No one was charged or went to jail," said the DFBI.

"We start out behind the eight-ball," the president concluded.

Next, Sybil met with her attorneys: White House Attorney, Lincoln Jukes, and Presidential Attorney Carter Anderton, and Roderick Michaelson, her private attorney.

"Gentlemen, I'm still mad. I want to move on the *Enquirer*. Please get together and finalize a letter on Roderick's letterhead stationery indicating our intent to sue. Make full use of DCIA Martin Obershauer's evidence. I want the plaintiffs to be me as a private person and me as the president of the United States. All three of you sign it, please."

"We're way ahead of you, Madam President," said Mr. Jukes with a bit of smug one-ups-man-ship lingering on his face. "Here is your copy."

Michaelson, Stonebridge, and Peekskill, Attorneys at Law

Chief Editor, *The Enquirer Magazine*
American Media Incorporated
1000 American Media Way
Boca Raton, Florida 33464

Clement Gioriani:

Sir: This letter will serve notice to you and your magazine that you are being sued in the District Federal Court of Washington, D.C., Judge Hickman Rogers III presiding. The plaintiffs are Sybil Norcroft Daniels, BS, MD, FACS, PhD, FAANS, current sitting president of the United States and her husband, Charles Middleton Daniels, the United States of America, and the Office of the President.

At issue is defamation of character of the plaintiffs. Be advised that the evidence against you and your magazine is ample for proceeding. Find enclosed excerpts from the formal evidentiary materials submitted to the court.

Depositions in the case will be held in the U.S. District Court for the District of Columbia, 333 Constitution Avenue N.W., Washington D.C. 20001, conference room 100. To assist you to find the site, be advised that the Courthouse is located at Third Street and Constitution Avenue, Northwest, Washington, D.C. one block west of the United States Capitol. Your deposition, Mr. Gioriani, is scheduled for Wednesday, December 23, 2022, six weeks hence.

Signed for the plaintiffs, President Sybil Norcroft Daniels and Charles Middleton Daniels

Roderick Michaelson, *Esq*. Personal Attorney at Law for the Daniels family, listed above
Signed for the plaintiff, The Office of the President of the United States of America
White House Attorney, *Lincoln Jukes, Esq.*

Signed for the plaintiff, Sybil Norcroft Daniels President of the United States of America
Chief Presidential Attorney *Carter Anderton, Esq.*
Dated: 10 November, 2022

Sybil agreed, and the notice was delivered by courier five hours later as if serving a warrant. Clement Gioriani had a standing order in his office that he was never to receive a summons. However, the hand selected server, Amos Claburn, did not just fall off the turnip truck. He chose a disheveled country hick look and told the two secretaries between him and Mr Gioriani's office that he had "the dirt on President Daniels and nudie pictures to prove it".

He was all the more convincing when he demanded a "million bucks" for what he had, which would be exclusive to the *Enquirer.*

"I'll take your information to Mr. Gioriani's office myself, Mr. Clayburn. You don't need to wait; we'll call you, don't call us."

"Ya'll kin call me Amos. I won't be 'Mr. Clayburn 'til I git the money from the boss. Make me wait five minutes more, and I'll take it ta the *In Touch* and *Life & Style* rags by late afternoon today. Which is it gonna be?"

Gioriani heard Clayburn–whose voice was stentorian–and was curious about what the hick had to offer. If it were nothing, he could dispense with the bother in a minute.

"Send him in," he ordered,

"This better be good," Gioriani said gruffly.

"Oh, Sir, it surely is. You Clement Gioriani, big boss of this here magazine?"

"The one and only."

He extended his hand to take the envelope Amos was holding. Amos quickly stepped forward, arm extended, and plastered the envelope on Gioriani's chest.

"You have been served, Gioriani."

Then Amos did a sharp about face and marched quickly out of the two offices. He paused only long enough to shed his wig and seedy plaid shirt into the waste basket as he exited.

Lieutenant General Mark A. Dietrich made a secure telephone call to Assistant to the President for National Security Affairs, LTG Hyrum Clussterson. It was flagged as "urgent".

"Hyrum, this is Mark. I have some good quality photos from NPIC [National Photographic Interpretation Center] to send you. They're hot off the griddle—less than an hour old."

Gen. Dietrich was the head of NGA [The National Geospatial-Intelligence Agency] a combat support agency under the United States Department of Defense and a member of the United States Intelligence Community, of sixteen coordinated agencies. Its primary mission is the collecting, analyzing, and distributing, of GEOINT [Geospatial Intelligence in support of National Security. NGA was known as the NIMA [National Imagery and Mapping Agency] until nineteen years ago, which was a reasonably good definition of its work.

The call originated from NGA headquarters— Campus East in Fort Belvoir North Area in Virginia.

Since 2018, researchers at the National Geospatial-Intelligence Agency became able to transmit a high-resolution terrain map capable of refining detail on a photograph from outer space down to the size of a car, and less. The process is complex, using photogrammetry, photo interpretation, geodesy, among other classified equipment and techniques, and requires fulltime dedicated officers and technicians. NGA's annual budget approaches $5 billion annually.

"Okay, Mark, it's your nickel, shoot."

"We have photos taken from way out in Tango Hotel Echo [space] that show in perfect detail, a set of launching units—an even dozen in number—being put into place as we speak in P'anmunjom-ni, North Korea. I hardly need to tell you that that spot is less than thirty miles from Seoul.

"Looks like ten of them have a target line directly at the capital of South Korea, and two are aimed at the Yellow Sea."

"Whiskey Tango Foxtrot! Apparently, they learned something from the last time around and hedged their bets—two big hits possible on our carriers when they arrive."

"Look, Hyrum, I'm privy to POTUS's general attitude towards belligerents who overstep. Do you think she would risk starting WW III if they fire a rocket?"

"If it is directed at us, the ROK, or Japan, yes. Your guys can trace a shot out into the ocean as a test run, can't they?"

"Sure they can. But will my guys have eyes on the right spots all the time?"

"I will pass it on to POTUS, but right now, focus on that area between P'anmunjom-ni, Seoul, and trajectories aimed at CONUS. I'll get you written authorization for the changes Victor Quebec [very quick]."

"Don't worry, it's only the fate of the world hanging from your shoulders, Hyrum. I have every confidence in you."

They laughed. A nervous laugh.

LTG Dietrich called Mrs. Carpentier to arrange for an emergency appointment.

"Push my schedule back an hour to accommodate the general, Mary. Get him in here ASAP," President Daniels asked her secretary.

"He's already in the White House; so, he should be not more than a jiffy."

Gen. Dietrich was a little out of breath when he was ushered into the Oval Office. He was carrying a blue folder in his left hand. He and the president shook hands.

"Thank you for getting here so promptly, General. Let's see what you have."

As he spread the NGA photos around on the Resolute Desk, Dietrich explained how they had been obtained and the location shown in the photographs.

"Stunning clarity, General. Give my congratulations to everyone in the NGA who had anything to do with these," Sybil said.

She studied them very carefully, using her desk magnifying glass. She quickly read the documentation for the imagery analysis from NIMA.

"That little…"

She stopped herself trying to keep to her vow not to be as foul-mouthed as some of her predecessors.

"They are poised to fire on Seoul and probably at us," Sybil said, pointing out the obvious. "So, General, is this another of Kim's big shows? Is he taunting us? Or is he so desperate in his weaselly little country that he might actually be ready to fire and to let the chips fall where they may?"

"All good questions, Madam President. Although he has bluffed in the past to extort money from us, you have made it clear that blackmail is not going to work in your administration. He obviously wants something… maybe another face-to-face with an American president to elevate his standing with the generals. We haven't heard any chatter about him being threatened with a coup of late.

"I will give you an opinion from our shrinks in the sixteen intelligence services: he's not suffering from any mental illness, except perhaps a case of having history's most colossal case of narcissistic, antisocial, and sociopathic, personality disorder. They believe that all three Kim dictators started out with Borderline Personality disorders as the underlying basis for their behavior. But, there is consensus; none of them–including the current Dear Leader–is delusional, has hallucinations, or does not have a grip on reality. In short, he's not crazy.

"Several of us, including the DNI, the DCIA, and the head of DARPA think this move has been done with such secrecy and is so well placed tactically, that we give it a greater than even chance that he is preparing a pre-emptive strike on Seoul under the presumption that you will not retaliate. This is based on some of his statements that he backed you down the last time he made threats; so, you don't have the spine to stop him. No insult intended, Ma'am."

"And none taken. Well, General, it is apparent that we have a situation on our hands. Please arrange for the usual suspects to gather in the Situation Room as quickly as possible and have this evidence ready at every chair. Thanks."

"I will make it happen and report back when the meeting is ready."

Because Sybil did not have enough misery already, the new FBI Director Horace Eyring caught her as she was exiting the Oval to go to the Situation Room.

"I'll be quick," he said, "the CSA is marching down Main Street in Atlanta. An elderly black man is standing right in the middle of the road with a placard that says, 'No more Slavery, No more confederacy, No more CSA.' The new confederates are unslinging their rifles. Looks like a show-down from which nothing good can come, Madam President. What do you want us to do?"

CHAPTER FIVE

The Situation Room was filled with officials and tension. Everyone looked to President Daniels to see what she was going to do. No one in that room doubted her "spine". But this was no ordinary day or ordinary situation. The question was not so much about starting WW III, but whether or not to wait or to make a single pre-emptive surgical strike.

LTG Dietrich stood with a long lighted pointer and showed the elements of the NIMA photographs pertinent to the questions at hand. Once oriented, most of the experts present could plainly see missile installations, mobile trucks to move their platforms about, artillery weaponry, cannons, two mechanized infantry divisions—the 108th and the 425th, and ground troops identified as the I Corps and the VII Corps.

Two photos from outer space actually showed persons guarding the weapons and technicians climbing around on the machinery, some with tools, and some with clip boards. It was a site of beehive level activity. One photo was so clear and precise that the Americans could all read a license plate on one of the trucks—clearly a DPRK military vehicle with the unmistakable license plate.

"Any questions? Any doubts?" Gen. Dietrich asked when he had finished his presentation.

Everyone shook his or her head.

"Madam President," he said as he sat down.

"Thank you General and everyone who worked to give this edge. I will render my judgment before we leave the room today; but, before I do, I want to hear your opinions. As always, agree, disagree, or admit that you don't know, but give me input."

Secretary of State Fiona Del Giordia spoke first, "Madam President, I am as astonished and dismayed as anyone in this room. I am fully aware of how rapidly those guns and missiles could reach Seoul and do catastrophic damage. But if we act in a hostile fashion, we are certain to set the spark off. I, for one, want to give diplomacy a chance."

"Do you have a specific plan, Madam Secretary?" the president asked.

"Not at the moment, but State can start to work on it right away."

"Madam Secretary, *this* is the moment."

The DOD, JCOS, and the heads of the missile commands, the USAF, and the theater commanders gave their opinions. There were differences of opinion, more about degree of response than whether to initiate military action.

President Daniels responded to their discussions with questions.

"It is decision time. Should we launch a pre-emptive strike? Should we warn first, wait until they react, and then either stand down or launch depending on their response, or should we take a step back and watch for now?"

The room became quiet. Many were holding their collective breaths.

The military officers huddled for five minutes, then the CJCS stood and acted in his role as spokesperson.

"We are unanimous: pre-emptive missile strike. No warnings, even to South Korea."

Secy. Del Giordia looked as if she wished to offer a rebuttal but thought better of it. She either changed her opinion or could see that the die was cast.

Sybil stood to give her answer, "Pre-emptive surgical strike, it is. I will contact President Park Chung IL-kwon to allow them to prepare, but he can be trusted to keep it secret and to move the project in the open as little as possible."

She turned to the CJCS and gave him an order, "General, prepare an immediate pre-emptive strike. Due to the Top-Secret nature of certain weaponry at your command, we will adjourn this meeting and you and I will agree on the precise orders."

When only the two of them remained in the room, the CINC said, "We cannot afford any time lapse between firing our weapon and their ability to react. Employ the resources of the Joint Services Space Command, and obliterate the military objective seen on those photographs. I know only generalities of the weapons; so, I will leave the details to you, Sir."

"Aye, aye, Madam President," he said.

"God save us all," Sybil said in parting.

The CJCS immediately contacted the commanders of the Joint Space Command.

"Generals and Admirals," he ordered the senior officers, "acting on orders from the CINC of the United States, you are hereby ordered to attack the site I have designated by its photographic and geophysical coordinates with all due speed. Employ the satellite RedEye Laser. Nothing is to be left alive or functional in those coordinates. Clear?"

"Aye, aye, Sir."

"Questions?"

"One, Sir. We all know that this will be the first time to use RedEye. Are we covered by the presidential order, including you? Who knows what could go wrong, and we will be launching without written orders?"

"You will get them, but fire on my orders now and trust me."

"May I speak candidly, Sir?"

"Speak."

"Do you trust the president that much? Our careers depend on her willingness to shoulder the responsibility."

"I do. She has our backs and will take any blame that falls. Trust her."

At 1106 EDT a red line of fire pierced the cloudless sky near the coast of the Yellow Sea in an arid beach sand and "coastal scrub"–soft chaparral and coarse clumps of stiff grasses–location in North Korea near the contested border with South Korea. After action space photographs revealed an area of burned sand littered with blackened body parts and destroyed machinery explosively disintegrated and consumed by fire. No living things were detected.

Missile batteries from north of the border commenced firing as soon as the North Koreans learned of the laser strike. Because the American president had forewarned the South Korean president, the "Iron Dome" missile and rocket defenses of the ROK took down all eighteen missiles fired at Seoul. A missile apparently aimed in the direction of Chicago, was blown to pieces before it could be fired.

The spokesman for the DPRK made an hysterical demand for United Nations action. The United States made no comment for five days, and then only gave a terse reply: "The United States denies all knowledge of any alleged attack against the Democratic Peoples Republic of Korea and further denies any allegations of complicity in any attack, if indeed one occurred."

Main Street, Atlanta, Georgia, April 12, 2022 was the scene of a tense drama occurring in double time. A well-disciplined 200-man military parade advanced on a lone man standing in the middle of the thoroughfare. He was seventy-two-year-old Daniel Beauregard Jones, an African-American veteran of Cold War combat action in Serbia. He was ram-rod stiff and held his neatly printed placard as if he were a union soldier with an American flag facing overwhelming odds against a confederate army armed with AR-16s. The paramilitary marchers came ever closer to the highly principled retired marine sergeant major, dressed in his uniform bedecked with campaign medals. The suit still fit perfectly. His boots were polished so highly that sun beams radiated off them.

The leader of the marchers brought the company to a halt.

"Move yer black butt outta here, now, Boy. We ah acomin' through whether y'all ah standing theayre ah not. Y'all understan' oah do Ah need to speak moah slowly so y'all kin git mah drift, Boy?"

Retired Sergeant Major Jones stood his ground and remained silent and still.

A police squadron raced to intervene.

Hearing the advance of the law enforcement officers, Caleb Danby Macomb, New Confederate Army captain, and the Man in Charge, gave loud orders:

"Front ranks assume combat firin' position!"

Twelve bearded and angry men took to one knee.

"Prepiah ta fiah!"

A squad of police vehicles screeched to a stop alongside the marchers. The officers began to rush from their vehicles.

"Fiah!!!" Macomb screamed, and Sergeant Major Jones was riddled with 187 bullets which ripped his chest to pieces.

A dozen television cameras, iPhones, amateur kodaks, and official police photographers, recorded the murder and created a martyr who would go down as a hero or an uppity scoundrel depending on who did the telling.

Sybil saw the event on television in real time as did more than 100 million other Americans and eventually billions of people around the world.

"Oh, no," she cried, expressing the first horrified sentiments of all those people.

"Get me FBI Director Horace Eyring, Mary," the president said as quietly as she could manage.

Mary Carpentier had been watching her iPad real time video of the events in Atlanta. She knew what her boss wanted, and she also knew that all hell was about to be unleashed.

Atlanta was not nearly the scene of chaos that DFBI Eyring had been expecting. The anticipated race riot had not happened because the early arrival of the municipal and then the state police had kept tempers, demonstrations, and counter-demonstrations, to a manageable minimum. The real—and nearly inexplicable—reason for the calm came from the CSA paradors, the murderers. The police on the scene rounded up the marchers, who submitted without even a murmur. Even the leaders—including "Captain" Caleb Danby Macomb—made no protest when they were searched for hidden weapons, read their Miranda rights, and hauled away in four prison buses with barred windows.

African-Americans might well have been expected to have erupted in protest against the senseless racially based killing of one of the most popular citizens of Atlanta. Seeing the docility and apparently easy confessions of the white murderers and hearing the calm explanations to the growing crowds about what had taken place, why, and where, the criminals were being taken, calmed the seething ire of the citizens of the capital city of all races and political leanings.

Eyring mused for a minute or two, rubbing his temples and the bridge of his nose to help to think, then observed to Atlanta FBI SAC Roswell Goodworth Viebel, "Pilgrim, it's quiet around here—too quiet."

He said it in his fairly accurate John Wayne impression.

"The CSA loonies have something up their sleeves. Maybe they think that cooperatively demonstrating willingness to follow the law will give 'em brownie points when they come before the judge. Maybe it's a kind of strategy to win the hearts and minds of the locals and even the Supreme Court when they have their secession hearing."

"Stranger things have happened," Eying pondered.

"Not much stranger," Viebel added.

Sybil stayed in contact with the FBI and local police agencies in Atlanta, with the intelligence services and military officers overseeing the North Korean tensions. So far, no further incidents had marred the quiet of either the Korean Peninsula or the old Confederate South. Whatever the motives or methods of her opponents were or how things would turn out, appeared to be a problem for another day. An old aphorism from her Sunday school days popped into her mind: "Sufficient unto the day is the evil thereof" said by Jesus in the Sermon on the Mount: Matthew 6:34. Sybil planned to leave those problems alone until they raised their ugly visages again.

CHAPTER SIX

At 4:36 EDT, the office of Michaelson, Stonebridge, and Peekskill, Attorneys at Law received a request for a conference call among Mr. Michaelson, and two attorneys for *National Enquirer Magazine*—Olympia Sessions and Bryan K. Denbow.

"What is the purpose of the call, Ma'am?" the firm's receptionist asked the secretary whose caller ID indicated that it came from Florida.

"Conference call," the Floridian with the Manhattan accent said brusquely.

"What is the call about, Ma'am? In order for any of our attorneys to engage, we must know what case is to be discussed, what the case number is, and who are the lead attorneys."

"I am calling from the office of the *National Enquirer*. That is all you need to know."

Judy Norton, the firm's receptionist had been told how to deal with this call, which was expected.

"That's the smut magazine?" Judy asked.

"Entertainment news, to be exact."

"My attorneys are very busy. Would you like to make an appointment?"

"Just arrange the stupid call!"

"Our hours are ten to five, week-days, closed on weekends. You said it was Mr. Michaelson you wanted to see? His next appointment is… let's see… three months… that would be February. We have a 4:15 opening that day. Would that suit your schedule?"

"Apparently, you don't know who you are talking to. I am calling for Clement Gioriani, the Senior Editor of one of the most powerful magazines in the world. Get me through to Mr. Michaelson's office, you moron!"

There was an audible click. The next three sentences from the *National Enquirer* went unheard, probably for the best because they were laced with profanity, blasphemy, obscenities, and scatological, references.

Half and hour later a second call came to Michaelson, Stonebridge, and Peekskill. This time it was a male voice.

"Hello, Ma'am, this is Bryan Denbow, how're you doing today?"

"Fine thank you, and you?"

"Also fine. I am calling about a matter of a threatened defamation suit filed by your Mr. Michaelson. It involves the White House."

"In what way?"

"Please, I don't want to be rude, but it is something best discussed by Mr. Michaelson, my partner Olympia Sessions who is of counsel for *National Inquirer Magazine*, and me. My name is Bryan Denbow. We are based in Boca Rotan, Florida."

"Oh, we had another call from your office this morning. Extremely rude. Am I to expect similar treatment from you, Sir? If so, we should just hang up, and you can take your business elsewhere. No member of this firm is expected to be subjected to abuse."

"I apologize for my receptionist. She has been discharged (a lie). Now can we get down to business— start over as it were?"

"What is the nature of your business? Do you already have a case file with us? If so, I will need the file number before I can communicate with Mr. Michaelson's office."

"I am calling to get the process started. This relates to a suit filed by Mr. Michaelson's client against our magazine."

"Oh yes. I knew there was a problem. Mr. Michaelson has just amended the filing to include Ickuello Longbright, the author of the article in question and against the photographer, whose name I can't pronounce."

"That is interesting but not why I am calling. We three attorneys need to talk before a scheduled deposition of our principle, Mr. Clement Gioriani."

"What shall I say is the issue for your client?"

"I presume you can guess that he is a very busy and very important man. He will not be able to come for a deposition in Washington DC on the scheduled date. Frankly, he just does not do depositions."

"I will relay your message, Sir; but the deposition is scheduled by the federal judiciary. They are awfully busy as well, as you can imagine; and, in my lengthy experience, they are not inclined to change dates. Failure to appear is a serious matter, and they are more likely than not to cancel your deposition altogether, charge you with failure, and either pursue criminal charges in court; or, the case of civil litigation, to find in favor of the party that showed up at their deposition. A word to the wise: they value punctuality."

"This is impossible, young lady. We need to negotiate. Please get me through to Mr. Michaelson… today if at all possible."

She promised to do that. Michaelson called the *Enquirer* office after seven in the evening, EDT. Since no one was in the office, he left a message for Mr. Denbow to call him the next morning at seven o'clock EDT.

Florida lawyers are loathe to begin business before ten. A common statement is "I don't stop throwing up until ten." But Denbow called back to Michaelson's office on time. The recorded message he received said, "Our office hours are ten A.M. to four P.M. Mondays through Fridays. No office hours on weekends or holidays."

Denbow's office staff shooed him out of the office to go soak in the cold swimming pool to calm down after that failed interchange.

Much as he hated to do so, Denbow had to report his failures to Mr. Gioriani. The Senior Chief Editor of the magazine made reference to Denbow's work ethic, competence, his mental capacity, and even his heredity, when the unfortunate man interrupted his morning private meeting with the new office girl.

Denbow was not fired but strongly urged to produce the desired results PDQ or he would be reassigned to the laundry room.

He sent a certified letter to be able to have a receipt for the sender–for an additional fee—and so he could receive a copy of the recipient's signature upon the recipient's receipt of the mail and detailed records of his mail's location. Mr. Denbow was an attorney, i.e. he trusted no one. He wanted registered mail because he did not trust the post office; registered mail is sent separately. Besides, important documents and valuables are usually sent through registered mail because it is more secure than certified mail.

The tracking revealed that he had put in the wrong zip code; to be fair, it was his secretary, and all she did was to invert two numbers of the zip. When he got that report, and after he calmed down, he wrote out the name, address, and zip code in block print, and arranged for a courier which required an additional telephone call and enduring a fairly lengthy wait while he learned the history of the particular courier service and about their sterling record.

The courier successfully delivered the letter. Roderick Michaelson received the message and sent back a reply.

> "Mr. Denbow, regrettably, no changes can be made in the place, time, and date of your client, Clement Gioriani's, deposition. We look forward to meeting him and you."
>
> Collegially yours,
> *Roderick Michaelson, Esq.*

For convenience, he added his direct office telephone information.

Denbow found himself at a loss for words—profanities, at least; and he barely tried. When he reported again to his boss, Mr. Gioriani, he found the Senior Editor did not have that limitation.

Next, he put in the first of two calls to Mr. Michaelson and learned that he was out for the day. He seethed but did not lose control. The following day, he was able to reach his adversary after two calls and a half hour wait.

"Good morning, Mr. Denbow. I'm glad we could finally get together. What can I do for you?" asked the cheerful and upbeat plaintiff's attorney.

"Change the date and Location of Gioriani's deposition."

"No can do."

"I'm telling you, Gioriani will never attend a deposition. It will be easier to get the president into a deposition that him."

"Hmmh, you do sound adamant. My client is equally adamant, I assure you. I believe she is highly desirous that court records are kept that may indicate criminal allegations which amount to threats. Money is not really her main goal. I will talk to her and see if there is anything that can be done by way of compromise. No promises, of course; she is her own woman; and I am a mere consultant in this process."

Denbow reported to Gioriani who calmed down long enough to say, "Get back to the lawyer and arrange a settlement negotiation. Losing in court would be an even worse disaster than when Carol Burnett beat us."

CHAPTER SEVEN

After her PDR with all of its foreboding information, Sybil's next meeting was with her three attorneys: Sybil's private attorney Roderick Michaelson, the presidential attorney Carter Anderton, and the White House attorney, Lincoln Jukes. The subject matter was to determine what the president really wanted, what she would settle for at a minimum, and how much publicity she was willing to have about the matter.

"My conversations with the *National Enquirer's* attorneys have made it clear that he wants nothing to do with actual courtroom appearances or depositions. For all of his bluster, he is most afraid of being convicted of a crime after a messy very public trial. He is a very rich and vain man. He can write off a high judgment cost on his and his company's IRS filings. We can force a hurtful high money ruling in our favor."

"Roderick, I have always said that money was not my object, not my reason for filing the suit... I've changed my mind. Have your conference and insist to the end on three things: the lowest money award I will accept is fifty million dollars but start at double. My other absolute is that he must print a full-page front cover retraction of the photo and admit in detail how it was fraud and photoshopping. Same for the beach photo with the Russian lothario. He must admit in a public nationwide television interview what he did, how he did it, and why. Finally–inside the same edition where he admits his wrongdoing on the front cover–I want a specific apology to me and my husband personally, to the presidency, and to the White House, separately and with different and appropriate language for each. Every retraction and apology must meet my final approval."

"That's a big ask."

"It has been an egregious injury."

Atlanta prepared for the "Trial of the Century"—the murder trial of the Confederate Army members who admitted to gunning down an African-American man in cold blood and without provocation. The city divided up along obvious political and ideological lines. There were tens of thousands of African-Americans who saw it as the case of the century for their anti-racism cause, and nearly equal numbers of Caucasians who saw it as the first in a number of *causes célèbres* to protect the white people who were being marginalized and for the large minority of whites who favored secession. Sybil's administration, the FBI, Georgia State, and Atlanta local law enforcement, and government officials, viewed the developing hostilities generated by the upcoming trials as impending severe internecine warfare in miniature with the capacity to grow ever wider.

Governor Lindsay called out the national guard; Mayor Dupres activated every law enforcement officer in the city—cancelled all leaves, days off, and vacations. The enforcement personnel were assigned to work twelve hour shifts as long as the trial lasted. The CSA and its militant arm—the New Confederate Army—was delighted. They could not have been happier if they had planned the entire publicity circus.

The comparable background–at least in its level of anger and racist thematics—occurred on November 14, 1960 in New Orleans. Leading up to that climactic day, was the ruling of *Brown v. Board* in which SCOTUS historically put down school segregation. Ruby Nell Bridges was a six-year-old African-American child whose mother wanted her to have the benefits afforded by a truly desegregated school. Near to the family's home was the all-white William Frantz Elementary school.

By the mere act of applying for Ruby to attend her neighborhood school, her father lost his job, the local grocery store stopped serving the family, and her sharecropper grandparents were turned off their land. Six-year-old Ruby was subjected to protests death threats from their neighbors. The previous year, Ruby attended the all-black segregated kindergarten class in an inadequate school with ill trained teachers.

The southern states united to resist integration anywhere, but especially in schools. A year later, however, a federal court ordered Louisiana to desegregate. The school district created entrance exams—only for African-American students—ostensibly to see if they were prepared to compete in a previously all-white school. Six African-American children–including Ruby–passed the test.

The furor was so great that her father began to resist having his daughter change to an integrated school, fearing for her safety. Her mother prevailed. The school district dragged its feet, delaying her admittance until November 14. Finally, Ruby Nell Bridges Hall was escorted by marshals and guardsmen to become the first African-American child to desegregate the all-white William Frantz Elementary School in Louisiana. She was to become the first African-American child ever in an all-white school.

Her father refused to be present, afraid of what might happen to his little girl. Ruby and her mother were escorted by four federal marshals to the school that first day and every day thereafter during that year. Ruby was awed by the size and grim determination of the marshals and the intimidating presence of national guard solders. She walked past crowds of angry whites—old and young, male and female–screaming vicious slurs at her. She later said that she only became frightened when she saw a woman holding a black baby doll in a coffin.

She spent her first day in the principal's office due to the chaos created as angry white parents pulled their children from school almost en masse. The most ardent segregationists withdrew their children permanently. Barbara Henry–a white Boston native–was the only teacher willing to accept Ruby; and all year, Ruby was in a class with a population of one.

Ruby ate lunch alone, never played with another student, and sometimes played with her teacher at recess. However, the courageous little girl never missed a single day of school that year.

Out in the crowd of whites–virtually frothing at the mouth–was a work gang of six inmates from the local jail. The heat and humidity were so stifling and wilting that a deputy sheriff guarding them collapsed. The inmates in their black and white striped jail garb could have taken the man's gun and driven away in the work van. However, they did the opposite. They used the deputy's phone to call the emergency line which saved the deputy's life. As a reward, the sheriff's office threw a pizza and homemade pie party for the six, and each was given a reduced sentence.

Weapons were brandished; the police and national guardsmen confiscated them despite screaming protests by the racist crowds. The African-Americans and the whites were kept separate to prevent killings and that was a close call.

The scene at the beginning of the trial of the CSA murderers was very much like that day back in November, 1960.

Judge Jimmy Carter Hodson gaveled the court to order and started the long and contentious process of *voir dire.* There were an even 300 potential jurors in the courtroom that first day, and it was only finally whittled down to the required fourteen—twelve jurors and two alternates—after ten grueling days of vetting the number from the ardent racists and equally determined anti-whites to seven African-American jurors and one alternate to five white jurors and one alternate. Hodson adjourned early on the final day of *voir dire*—a Friday—to allow the sizzling tension in the courtroom to cool down over the weekend.

Sybil watched and waited tensely knowing that this might well turn out to be a precedent setting case in the march towards the Supreme Court and a decision determining the 2022 or 2023 version of the secession question—on her watch.

An extraordinary meeting of the State Affairs Commission of the Democratic People's Republic of Korea–formerly known as the NDC [National Defense Commission]—deemed by the elite to be the supreme national defense leadership institution of state power, the armed wing of the Worker's Party of Korea which—under their Songun policy–was the central institution of North Korean society. It was attended in North Hamgyong province with the *Highest Dignity*—First Chairman—attending. The position of president of North Korea had been removed the previous month by the Highest Dignity.

The extraordinary nature of the meeting was that it was taking place at a nonplanned date, because the nation feared that the Dear Leader Kim Jong Un had died in a surgical accident during the past month, and because of the unproved–but presumed–US attack on North Korean installations.

As all the senior officers in the several military units alighted from their vehicles, they took note of the impressive array of anti-aircraft guns pointing at stacks of baled hay, one for each gun. The precision of the array and the shiny cleanliness was impressive as would be expected by the Great Father of the People.

The high-ranking authorities sat in serried rows, as nearly as possible in order of rank. They sat in silent awe awaiting the emotionally charged moment when he should grace them with his august presence.

As they should have expected, Highest Dignity and First Chairman stepped onto the dais and walked to the podium exactly on time. The hall burst into a frenzy of clapping, cheering—and shortly—weeping with joy upon seeing him. He raised his hand, and the hall became silent except for a few snuffles coming from the most senior of the military officers.

"My people, my generals, I have come to tell you several truths which you will take to your innermost centers," the thirty-seven-year-old Supreme Leader began.

No one failed to note what an auspicious occasion they were experiencing. First Chairman Kim's perfectly tailored uniform was bedecked with his medals and badges of honor—several counted over fifty of them. They lined each side of his chest in three rows reaching from just below his clavicles to his belt line. It was also noted that he had more medals than any other man in the room, including those who were twice his age.

He continued, "We have endured a difficult period recently. Lies have been spread about my incapacitation. You see the falsehood of that by the fact that I stand here perfectly healthy, in an excellent state of fitness, and with my genius mind functioning fully. Because of those lies, some sitting in this room plotted to overthrow me and the Workers Party of Korea and to assume power and control. That did not happen, and those who connived are hereby convicted of treason and will be dealt with as all traitors should under our law.

"We were attacked without provocation by that blond girl who somehow accomplished a coup in the United States and has taken over the reigns of government. We must make them pay, but in my wisdom, I shall forebear a great nuclear attack on the American lackies to the south of us, but instead will hurt and annoy the entity we all know pulls the puppet strings.

"I have ordered one half of the NKSOF [North Korean special operation force] 100,000 men and women, to arrange covert and clandestine black ops in the United States. Our Korean People's Army Special Operation Force consists of the world's best and most specially equipped and trained elite military units are trained to perform military, political, and psychological, operations for the Motherland. They shall creep into that devil's country as quiet as fog. They will enter undetected. I tell you that this is a new and perfectly functioning spearhead of North Korea. The elite SOF—the Lightning Commandos unit—was created by me to counter the U.S. Navy SEALs. I assure you that our secret army will overwhelm the obscenely arrogant American military and put those SEALs to shame before all the world.

"The KPA Navy has 24 Romeo class diesel electric submarines. These submarines have been used primarily in coastal areas against our neighboring enemy and are an excellent platform to deposit units offshore. They shall accomplish the task and make it possible for our world's best SOFs to put the Americans into panic and chaos. I predict here and now that we will seat a new president in Washington, one who does our bidding."

He rested his voice and looked out over the crowd to see if he could catch anyone asleep. Everyone in the room remained in rapt attention even though he was no longer speaking. He took a hearty drink from his personal metal water container, emblazoned with his name and list of earned medals.

"I will now direct you concerning several items of business and change for the ruling class and for the country. Do not interrupt.

1. "We shall enact military ranks higher than general. The first is Field Marshall, and I have been appointed the first Field Marshall by the National Defense Commission of the Democratic People's Republic of Korea, I am pleased to announce."

   There was considerable fidgeting in the ranks to stifle the desire to shout, clap, and even to dance in celebration. But the Great Leader had given an order, and he would not allow anyone to act outside that order.

2. "We hereby rescind the decisions and directives of state organs that run counter to the orders of the chairman of the National Defense Commission of the Democratic People's Republic of Korea and

to the decisions and directives of the National Defense Commission acting together.

3. "North Korea appoints our fine ex-army officer General Ri Son-gwon as the new foreign minister. This appointment of comes as I realize that a much tougher stance on nuclear talks must be taken with the United States.

4. "As of today, Pyongyang declares that it is no longer bound by its self-imposed moratorium on long-range ballistic missile and nuclear tests.

5. "Now comes the joyous part of this meeting— both for me and for you.

Two men brought their hands up from their laps where they had been resting reverentially and made as if to clap. A general on either side them put a quiet hand on each of the fool's forearms and forestalled the likely disastrous action, however well intentioned.

"I shall award those deserving heroes and patriots with tokens of the nation's pleasure."

The process took three hours because there were a great many men present, and because each man received multiple medals and commemoratives. Looking at the generals, it would have been most difficult to find a location on the chest of his uniform where he could put even one new medal; but they all succeeded. Not to do so would have been an instance of Lèse-majesté.

Considering the fact that–except for some minor military support for the Ethiopian Civil War in the early 1990's–North North Korea has not fought a single major conflict since the early 1950's during what the Americans call the Korean War. Although there have been minor incursions in the South, very few North Koreans were ever involved at any given time. Nevertheless, there a myriad of honors commemorated on military uniforms. In the assemblage of that meeting most had more than thirty, and some had more than forty-five.

In his droning high little voice Kim Jong Un called out for each man in his turn to come to the dais to receive his honors.

To one, he would announce, "I hereby award *Attentiveness Award*—this award is for listening to the Supreme Leader for numerous hours with full attention; the Order of the National Flag, 1st Class, awarded under the criteria of the Soviet Order of the Badge of Honor. This award is presented to a man who exemplified himself in the fields of Science, Economics, and teachings of Socialist Ideologies. [technically, the man had never finished his university degree]; and the Order of Korean Labor for efficient and meritorious professional labor." [he was a professional soldier, and coincidentally, a second cousin of chairman Kim's].

To another he would announce the awarding of the North Korean Competence Medal. It was awarded for "appearing capable in performing your duties." [Failure to appear competent can lead to death—South Korean news reported that 'North Korean Leader Kim Jong-un Executes a Turtle Farmer For 'Incompetence'.", VICE News]. That man's award would also include the Order of the National Flag 2nd Class, the Soldier's Medal of Honor 2nd Class for acts of individual gallantry in combat. The insignia design is similar to the Soviet Union Order of the Red Star. The Dear Leader did not elaborate, nor did he mention that the last military action by North Korea occurred fifty years previously.

Another would be called to the dais and presented to his comrades to receive four medals at once: Order of Colliery Service Honor 2nd Class, the Order of Freedom and Independence 1st Class [originally given to Division, Corps, or Army field commanders for achievement in battle, later for lower formation commanders for skill in battle, and still later—under Kim Jong Un—for political valor; Order of Fishery Service Honor 2nd Class; and the Partners in Peace Award [a popular award is given to those who had any contact with American basketball player Denis Rodman while he was in North Korea during several trips. Kim Jong-un valued Rodman because he "appeared like the average American–facial piercings jewelry, tattoos, sunglasses worn inside buildings, bleached hair, odd arrogant behavior. The Dear Leader uses Denis's image regularly to show North Koreans what average Americans look like.

After hours of being witness to such significant awards, the grand finale at last allowed intense emotion to be displayed with loud and prolonged clapping, open weeping, casting one's body to the floor in an expression of ecstasy, and moaning out the Great Leader's many titles. Kim Jung Un awarded himself: The Heavenly Cow Award—this award was for all military officers that would also partake of Kim Jung-II's favorite meat, the donkey [neither spoken of tongue-in-cheek nor greeted with smiles]; the Brilliant Leader Worship Award for those who come up with the most creative compliments and praises; The Hero of the Republic Award, the highest award of the Democratic People's Republic Of Korea until the Order of Kim Il-Sung was established in 1972 awarded for extreme heroic exploits during war. Kim Jong Un awarded himself both medals for the sake of efficiency and completeness. [It was not mentioned that Kim had never been anywhere near a battle. In South Korea, detractors irreverently called it the "Whose Your Daddy Award"]; and the Eating Well Award for securing better rations. It is awarded for every three years of prosperity in food consumption. Kim wears three of those medals. [It was not mentioned that more than half of the rank and file soldiers live near starvation].

For reasons not elaborated upon, Kim awarded himself the Order of Military Engineering Service Honor 10 Years. [In October 2006, when Kim Jong-un was in his early twenties and still two months away from his graduation from Kim Il-Sung Military University, he was given his diploma with honors. Throughout his education from childhood on, he never took exams, got exam results, or matriculated in difficult subjects like engineering].

A general behind Kim signaled that the award ceremony was over. The audience—as if of one accord—expressed their great admiration and joy by weeping, fainting, writhing, and convulsing with near multiple-orgasmic joy–feigned or not.

However, the grand meeting of the senior military officers of the DPRK was not yet over. Perhaps, it could be said that the most exciting parts were yet to come.

CHAPTER EIGHT

America's only deep agent within the NDC [National Defense Commission] was able to smuggle his report out to South Korea and thence to the CIA. The spy was able to list some—but not all—of the medals and awards given out during that extraordinary meeting in North Hamgyong Province. He related that he, himself, was given the Order of Freedom and Independence 2nd Class; *Kim Jong-II Railroad Award* [for senior officers that accompanied The Dear Leader on train trips since the Respected Leader had a fear of flying and refused to fly—a state secret], Medal For Military Merit, Amazing Execution Award [given to military officers who come up with interesting and creative ways to execute North Koreans.

It has also been awarded to those who participate in these bizarre executions], and Supreme Gulag Award [given to officers affiliated with the massive gulag system where 200,000 North Koreans are imprisoned for dissent, etc.]. The agent insisted that he had never had anything to do with the gulags; they were not part of his MOS. He also received the Commemorative Order of the 40th Anniversary of Fatherland Liberation War Victory for the third time.

Of more immediate significance in the deep agent's report was his revelation that Kim had gathered the entire audience and marched them out to the adjacent open field where the odd array of anti-aircraft guns was stationed. He ordered the military police to arrest eleven members of the group of generals and to tie them face forward to the piles of baled hay a hundred yards distant from the guns.

They were thus executed for the crime of having made false reports that "enraged" leader Kim Jong-un and had been discovered by the DPRK internal security agency. In addition, every family member of every criminal "false reporter" was executed in the Rungrado 1st of May Stadium. The deep agent discovered that the false reports referred to were that the *Utpun* [Superior Person] had been gravely ill after surgery. And, the Fearless Leader of the Nation, declared that he had ordered a missile attack against the continental United States of America.

The final convincing display put on by the Highest Dignity caught the assembled generals completely by surprise. When the smoke from the antiaircraft gun reprisals cleared, Kim made a slight gesture of raising his right index finger. Immediately a team of guards brought out a tall wire fence enclosure and placed it mid-center in front of the crowd. They left and quickly returned with an animal transport truck full of large starving dogs. The dogs were dumped into the enclosure and tormented by throwing in a few handfuls of raw pork meat.

Kim made announcement: General Kyŏng Chin-Mae has been convicted of attempting to overthrow the state. He merits special execution."

Gen. Kyŏng was force marched to stand in front of the howling dogs. He was then stripped naked. He stood quivering and crying until the guards lifted him bodily and threw him over the high woven wire cage. The ravenous dogs that finished the man until only bony scraps remained. His large nuclear and extended family joined those of the "false reporters" in Rungrado 1st of May Stadium. Lesson conveyed.

The deep agent was one of the most trusted agents in the entire CIA repertoire and a personal friend of the president of the ROK [Republic of Korea]. Sybil had no choice but to accept the message to be of A+ quality. She ordered the entire defense alert system to go to DEFCON 3, to send the other two carrier squadrons to Korean waters, and all US military agencies and personnel on land, on the sea, and in the air, near the Korean peninsula to be placed on DEFCON 5.

After discussion with the PM of Canada, she ordered the same for NORAD [The North American Aerospace Defense Command, a bi-national United States and Canada organization charged with the missions of aerospace warning, aerospace control, and maritime warning, for North America]. She clamped a lid of secrecy on all matters pertaining to the North Korean Hermit Kingdom and about all the defense preparations she had ordered.

And the day had barely begun.

She had not even been able to leave the Situation Room after the preparations for what the glum keepers of the secret viewed as the forerunner of WW III. The next chapter for the day was a riot in the streets of Atlanta—apparently organized by the CSA despite all its pretenses of peaceful, orderly, and lawful intention. It was beginning to spread to the capitals of the old Confederate South. Sybil, DOD officials, the JCOS, and the Attorney General's Office, began to light up the airways communicating with state officials. She and they were all determined that this action would not turn out to be a second chapter of the recent ugly insurgency in the country.

The Southern Council of Churches [which did not include Catholics, Jews, Hindus, or Muslims] declared the day to be a regional day of prayer and implored the rest of the Christians of the country to join them. In every state involved, the national guards were called up. Police, sheriffs, and university police, were put on full alert for the duration. Obviously armed patrols began to travel the streets—including several unauthorized units wearing confederate uniforms and better armed than the authorized law enforcement groups.

Inside the United States Federal Courthouse in the Richard B. Russell Federal Building on 75 Ted Turner Drive, SW, Atlanta, there was no physical acting out. Opening arguments could hardly be described as cordial or even polite, but Judge Jimmy Carter Hodson was bound and determined not to let any of the "tomfoolery" outside to contaminate his courtroom or his jury. He had warned any and all that if even the slightest disturbance got into his courtroom, he would close the court to spectators; and if the marshals of the court could not easily handle any situation, he would sequester the jury and the lawyers for the duration. Everyone in the stolid, white, multi-story block house of a building was a bit subdued at that threat.

The Atlanta Attorney's Office was headed by Jacob Ryan Scottalia, and today he sat first chair as the federal prosecutor. He and four other US attorneys occupied the prosecution seats representing the government's interests. Scottalia gave the first argument to the jury because the prosecution—not the defense–must prove the case.

"Ladies and gentlemen of the jury, my name is Jacob Ryan Scottalia. I am the attorney for the people of the United States of America. I represent the individuals described in the Constitution as 'We the People'. This is a trial about a man who was murdered and taken from his loving family. It is about a group of men who are today on trial for their lives. As is abundantly obvious, this is a most serious activity; and I thank you for doing your civic duty by being here and ask that you give heed to what I am about to tell you."

He took a moment to look directly into the eyes of each juror in turn. His gaze punctuated the strong level of feeling and emotion he felt.

"While it is possible that you have heard or seen in the media something about this case. I ask you to ignore whatever you have heard and to make your important judgment based only on the *evidence presented here* in this court. I intend to introduce the themes of this case which are pertinent. The prosecution will be as concise and direct as possible in order to help you to understand what was done, to whom, for what reason; and to urge–after you have heard all of the evidence–that you should find these defendants guilty.

"This is not about politics or ideology other than as a means of understanding what was done. It is not about history of the old South or a desire to return to antebellum times. It is about murder with malice aforethought, conspiracy to commit murder, and racial hatred. Make no mistake, this *is* a hate crime with many defendants—200 to be exact. We will introduce witnesses and evidence to prove to you beyond a reasonable doubt that this crime was committed, that it was committed by these defendants there on the left side of the court room where you are seated, and that it was the product of an active and ongoing conspiracy. When all is said and done, the case is simple; it is specific to the murder of this victim, seventy-two-year-old retired Sergeant Major Daniel Beauregard Jones, an African-American veteran of Cold War combat action in Serbia, a husband to Ruby Sapphire Jones, father of eight children, and grandfather of fourteen…"

He paused for effect.

… "and it was a hate crime. Mr. Jones was an African-American—a pillar of this community–and the color of his skin was the only offense he gave to a group of hateful racists. Our evidence will include three witnesses of the crime itself, three witnesses of the planning and conspiracy, and three witnesses as to the mind-set of hate that underlay the killing of Mr. Jones.

"After we have presented the witnesses and documentary evidence Ladies and Gentlemen of the jury, we will ask you to find each and every one of these defendants guilty as charged of each count in the indictment. This is about a capital crime, and we will ask you to bring back a recommendation that these men be executed for their crimes…

Again, he fixed his eyes on those of the raptly attentive jury.

"You are sworn to do your duty, to pay attention to the evidence, to be triers of the facts. Then, you will be asked to bring back the only verdict that is reasonable in this case. Thank you."

After Mr. Scottalia returned to his seat, Judge Hodson, said, "Mr. Lee, for the defense."

Mr. Lee was a ram-rod stiff, slender, man of six-feet-seven inches tall. He had a patrician carriage, a lean and hungry looking face, a short neatly trimmed mustache and a long head of snow-white hair. He was dressed in a light grey three-piece suit, wore a prominent gold pocket watch across his chest, and a large Christian cross around his neck. His tan shoes were obviously hand-made and polished to a gleam. He wore a strong yellow polka-dot power tie.

"Mah friends, Ladies and Gentlemen of this fahn jury, allow me to introduce mahself. Ah am Robert Alfred Lee, of Etlana, foah the defense. Ah am heah to correct erroahs about the way this unfoatunate case has been depicted in the anti-South press and heah in this coaht tahdahy.

"This case is about an oppressed people sticking up foah theah raghts as citizens of these United States, who have be-en so toahmented by impropah laws and unfair advantages given tah scahtan people wi-ath privileges, that they felt duty-bou-und tah assert theah inalienable raghts as set asade in ouah Constitution—includin' laef, libaty, and the puhsuit of theah happiness. They were engaged in a pahfectly peacable mahch to make cleeah theah Constituionally pro-tected raghts, and beliefs tha-at everah American cherishes in his or huh bosom."

"Mah friends, yah'all may not quite agree with my fellow southerners heah, but that does not make anah kinda mattah. They woah exercisin' theah raghts… their raghts as Americans. Y'ah'll will learn that they ahah membahs of the Confederate States of Ahmerica, a legitimate pooliticaly pahty in these heah United States, and that they wish to have the coahts allow them to secede from this union that does not seuve them as it does some othahs in the country who have assumed to take majoritah raghts upon themselves even though theyah the minority. A rabble-rousah made a public spectacle of himseff and taunted these ahdent southen boahs, causin' a ruccus that lead to the unfoatunate shootin' of that man.

"No one can say who pulled the triggah fust. It could wella come frum the crowd of Afric-aan-Americans along the parade route. Although we ahah not required to do so, mah team and ah will introduce a witness who saw just such a man do so. You understan' that that constitutes reasonable doubt. When you heah out oah witness you will noah that you must acquit these defendants, friends of mahn over theah. That's all we ask of yah'all."

"Now, Ah can tell yah'all that more'un a coupla mah boahs took lah-detectah tests and passed 'em wi-th flyin' collahs, but that evidence was refused bayh the coaht."

"Objection, the defense attorney is presenting argument as if it were evidence, your Honor," the US Attorney interjected.

It is unusual for opposing attorneys to object to anything in their opponent's opening or closing statements, but Mr. Scottalia was not about to allow inadmissible statements as if they were evidence without having the jury be informed.

Judge Hodson said to Mr. Lee, "That is a correct statement, Mr. Lee, but you may not make it in this court. The jury will disregard the statement about lie detector tests, also known as polygraph tests. Such tests are inadmissible in any court in the land. However, you may continue your opening, Mr. Lee. I will choose to regard your hasty statement as mere enthusiastic rhetoric, strong advocacy, and excusable hyperbole, as found in the Baldwin case. Carry on now Mr. Lee but mind you stay away from attempting to present evidence that you do not intend to substantiate."

"Mah apologies, Yoah Honah. Won't happen again, Sah.

"It comes from mah haht that Ah will present evidence excusin' these enthusiastic southern boahs of committin' any crime othah than bein' white in a political correctness wurld. You will recognize that theah is more than reasonable doubt heah, that no one of these boahs can be identified as the shooter of that black rabbler rouser, let alone that all them did so actin' togethah.

That bein' so, you must acquit them once yah'll see the totality of the evidence."

Sybil had her own monitor, but her presence during the zoom conference between all three of her lawyers, and those of the senior editor of the *National Enquirer Magazine*—a fact noted soberly by all attendees. After introductions, Clement Gioriani, the editor himself, made a short statement, "I will never settle."

CHAPTER NINE

The voice of Bryan Denbow, Clement Gioriani's soft spoken attorney could be heard in the background beseeching his boss to leave the legal negotiations to the attorneys. His outbursts were only creating useless animosity. It must have worked because Gioriani's voice was not heard again in the ensuing conversations. All participants were dressed in their Sunday best, and were also wearing their best facial expressions and decorum.

"So, Bryan, you asked for this electronic face-to-face conversation. Why don't we let you say your piece? offered Roderick Michaelson, President Daniels's private attorney.

"Look, Guys, I know what my client said. He's mad, and he's acting with his usual bluster. Actually, he is paying us to negotiate. You have made a first proffer–$100 million with nothing said about having an NDG [Non-Disclosure Agreement]. I don't think anyone here believes that that is anything more than wishful thinking on the president's part. What do you say, why don't we get down to something sensible?"

"Bryan, let me tell you who you are dealing with. President Daniels is ordinarily quite affable, willing to compromise, and can see the other side's point-of-view. But, I have to let you know that for her this is nothing ordinary. The magazine has attacked her personally, her family, her very precious reputation, her presidency, and her ability to negotiate with friends and enemies—especially enemies. Her anger is a cold sort of thing.

No doubt you recall her recent handling of the insurgency, her employees who committed felonies, the English who threatened and injured us, and the North Koreans who posed an existential threat. Believe you me, the *National Inquirer* and its editor, Clement Gioriani, is right up there on her badness list. She has ice water for blood and bulldog DNA when it comes to a fight. She–in very fact–does not give up. That is how she got to where she is… Can she compromise? I wouldn't swear to it, but I will talk to her like a wise and experienced old uncle about some kind of compromise and will get back to you."

"Let's make it soon, Roderick. It does neither party to this for it to drag on and to develop moment in the press."

"You mean, like the *National Enquirer*?"

"No, I *don't mean* that. There is enough bad press about the nation's number one celebrity news magazine already. Gioriani's main goal in even talking about this fiasco with you guys is to get it to go away."

"Oh, Bryan, my executive assistant has contacted the busy president. She sent a pretty simple message, and I quote, 'Make me an offer I can't refuse.' My interpretation is that she has thrown down the gauntlet. I strongly suggest that you get back with an offer that will pique her interest. She has all the power of the presidency and is not afraid to use it. I tell you simply, that power is beyond the imagination of your Mr. Gioriani."

"I'll tell you up front and in all candor that I am authorized to offer three things: a monetary settlement of $2 million, an iron-clad non-disclosure, non publicity clause, and no apology of any kind ever. Take it or leave it, and we'll see you in court. That is a quote as well—although I admit I omitted some adjectives."

"Then, we're done for today. I will forward your information to the president. She won't give it a moment's thought; that is a given—any of it. We will move on with our plans for a federal trial in Washington. Better hope your friendly Mr. Gioriani has some powerful friends here."

"Look, Roderick, don't be too hasty. I'm sure there's a compromise somewhere down the line that we just don't see quite yet. Really, I have a question, is the Lady really that cold? Really that vindictive?"

"Let me put it this way. I remember once when she was the DCIA, and she had to track down a traitor to this country who had killed a dear friend of hers. She caught the criminal and insisted on handling the matter in-house. The criminal disappeared from public view; and, when the DFBI was queried about what she had done, he said, 'that lady believes that revenge is like vichyssoise; both are better served up cold.' I repeat myself; she never quits. You can pass that along to your client who believes that he has great influence, power, and can stare down this president."

While her attorneys were dealing with the *National Enquirer*, President Daniels was getting regular briefings on the trial procedures on Atlanta and about the red hat, grey coat riots beginning to pop up in major cities across the US. She was impressed with the resources this hate group had.

The federal prosecutor produced three citizen witnesses of unimpeachable credibility regarding who fired the weapons that took the life of retired Sergeant Major Daniel Beauregard Jones. Two statements will suffice, because they were very much the same.

> Q: Mr. Courtney, please tell the jury what you saw on the day in question that was out of the ordinary.
>
> A: Well, we don't much git parades in Atlanta, and never ones by confederate soldiers nowadays. But that weren't the real unusual thing. What I seen was this old vet standin' stock still in the middle a Main Street at attention like a proper soldier. He was holdin' a placard on a stick."
>
> Q: What did the placard say, Mr. Courtney?
>
> A: It says in big, clear block letters, "NO MORE CONFEDERACY. NO MORE SLAVERY. EVER."
>
> Q: What happened next?
>
> A: Well, Sir. Them guys in the uniforms ran down the street towards the old vet, dropped into some sorta firing position, and blew him to pieces. He

was defenseless and did not do nothing to them guys whatever. Worst thing I ever seen."

The next witness was also a direct witness of the crime and one of the arresting officers. His name was Rodger Coleman Badger, Atlanta Municipal Police sergeant.

Q: Sergeant, thank you for your careful description of the activities on Atlanta's Main Street that day.

A: I was one of a fairly large contingent of state, local, and federal, law enforcement officers assigned to prevent or respond to any kind of violence. Up to the moment, the confederate club members saw the victim, retired Sergeant Major Daniel Beauregard Jones, standing in the middle of the street in was all peaceful and nice like.

Q: We have established that he was carrying a placard with block print pleading with the public and the marchers—I guess—not to continue preaching a gospel of hatred towards blacks, not to work to reinstate slavery, and to stop preaching about the idea that lynching was all right.

A: That's right. When the marchers were half a football field away from the man, they could have easily gotten police assistance by simply turning their heads one way or another. They did not do that.

Q: What *did* they do?

A: I tell you, members of the jury, I was stunned. The pseudo-confederates started running towards the deceased screaming and yelling anti-Negro slurs, hate messages, and cursing him. He took it like a real man. Just stood his ground. I knew the guy in charge that day; name's "Captain" Caleb Danby Macomb. He was no more of a captain than I am. That so-called Confederate Army has more colonels that the Italians do. He and I went to high school together. He started shouting orders for the men to rush Sgt-Maj Jones, then the command to shoot him down, which they did. I tell you, Counselor, every mother's son of them shot that poor man. I was the arresting officer that put the cuffs on Macomb.

The testimonies of the next three witnesses called by the prosecution can be summed up by the sworn statements of Agnes Brown, landlady of the deceased, and part of the same community development group as him.

Q: Mrs. Brown, would you please tell the jury what you know about retired Sergeant Major Daniel Beauregard Jones?

A: Good a man as ever there was. He pays his rent right on time, every time, helps out the local kids who get into trouble, helps 'em with their school work, goes to the Big Bethel AME Church on 220 Auburn Ave NE, every Sunday and is onna the deacons there. It's where I go, too."

Q: Does he have a criminal record or a history of being a trouble-maker?

A: Just the opposite. He's squeaky clean, got kinda a Boy Scout way about him—you know, lives all those scout laws all'the time. The local po-olice comes to him to help find bad guys, help the good'nes, and takes in mixed-up kids. He's a history kinda guy, always readin' about the Civil War, and slavery, and the lynchin's. That kinda thing. He's like a professor. Real smart.

The court adjourned for the day half an hour after the usual closing time. The following day, the prosecution dealt with the issue of this having been a hate crime. Two testimonies will be all that is necessary of the three the prosecution questioned.

The first was a continuation of Agnes Brown's testimony.

Q: Mrs. Brown, did Mr. Jones ever indicate to you that he hated white people?

A: No, Sir, never. He did not hate nobody. Nice to everyone he seen. Got along fine with the white folk in the neighborhood. Not a mean bone in his body.

Q: But, Mr. Jones was carrying a sign when he was shot. Are you familiar with that?

A: Sure am. Seen him make it and seen him acarryin' it, proud and determined as punch.

Q: Wasn't that a hate sign?

A: Certainly was not. He was a real student of slavery, and he did not want anyone to get it started again in the south or anywhere else, for that matter. Sergeant Jones was actin' like a determined preacher. He was very well aware of what those CSA trash stood for. They had hate signs all over the place that day. I took a buncha pictures on my cell phone. You turned 'em all in to the court; don't you remember?

Q: I didn't forget. And now its time to have them listed as Prosecution Exhibit 13E.

In keeping of having his prosecution short and simple, but telling, the prosecution produced three more witnesses—to make the final point of the indictment, that this was indeed a hate crime to which could be attached special circumstances leading to attachment of the death penalty to a guilty verdict. The first witness to that effect was, State Trooper Lieutenant Thomas Calhoun who was present at the parade on the fateful day directing his troopers on how and where to stand and how to keep their cool in case violence broke out.

Q: Lieutenant Calhoun, we have had ample testimony about what happened; I mean, about the murder of Sergeant-Major Jones. I have questions for you related to the possibility that this was a hate crime. First, Lieutenant, could you overhear the comments coming from among the parade spectators and from the marchers?"

A: Yes, Sir. I was less than four feet from both of those lines of people.

Q: Would you characterize them, give examples, that sort of thing to the best of your recollection?

A: I could hear them just fine, and I do recollect what was said. The spectators were mostly black people. They weren't shouting, or cursing, or calling anybody names. Quite a few of them were saying "Shame, shame on you," and saying that to a particular white guy they seemed to know. Now the confederate marchers were quite another thing. They yelled stuff at the black folks that'd make the Devil blush—swearing, name calling, screaming—literally screaming—nasty stuff about lynching, the coming back of slavery, making whores out of their women and baby girls. The word "hate" must have been used close to a thousand times by those two hundred men and their leaders. I was humiliated for my race. The second witness for that phase of the prosecution's case was Caleb Danby Macomb, himself.

Q: Mr. Macomb, have you been given any incentives by the government for your testimony here today?

A: I demand to be identified by my rank of captain in the New Confederate Army. I am a prisoner of war.

Q: That remains to be adjudicated, Sir. However, I will call you "captain" for now. Please tell us about any incentives.

A: The death penalty was removed from any sentencing.

Q: Tell the jury about your current occupation.

A: I am proud to serve as a captain in the New Confederate Army, the liberators of the south and the means of returning it to its antebellum glory. They pay my wages, and I serve the cause.

Q: Did you participate in a parade down Atlanta's Main Street on April 12, 2022?

A: I am proud to say that I did in fact lead that military parade.

Q: What was the purpose of that "military" parade?

A: Show the government of America that the CSA is serious about secession, put the mud people in their places, and to start a riot if possible, but make it appear to be instigated by the mud people and their traitor-white servants.

Q: Tell the jury what plans you made to carry out those intentions.

A: We were going to find an angry and shouting black and attack him and turn it into a riot. Turns out, this one old mudder made that easy. He was standing smack dab in front of our march and taunting us. So, I took advantage of the opportunity and ordered a charge, then for my front ranks to assume the position and clear the line of march.

Q: How, exactly, was that accomplished?

A: I ordered all troopers to fire their automatic weapons in defense of our flag and our country. They all sprayed him with AR-16 fire.

Q: Forensics found that the man sustained 183 gun-shot wounds. Did you consider it necessary to use such excessive force?

A: Certainly. One bullet to wipe him from the earth, and 182 to show the used-up nation of the USA that we will be given our freedom, or we will fight. It will be the second "War for Southern Independence", and the names of our 200 soldiers marching that day will go down in history as heroes of that independence movement.

Q: Did African-Americans or anyone commit violence against you or your men before or after your action?

A: Don't be ridiculous. You are talking about mud-people. They can't fight. Nosiree, we got the jump on them, according to plan, and took out the leader. We made our point.

Q: Do you have any regrets or wish to express remorse?

A: Not for a second. And I speak for all my good strong white men.

Sybil and her cabinet sat spellbound at the testimonies they were hearing.

"Not to be dramatic, my friends and fellow servants of America; but any effort to circumvent the law to have a single city, state, or region secede from the union will have to be over my dead body. It looks like we are going to see blood shed in our streets. I am beginning to understand what Abraham Lincoln and his 'Team of Rivals' cabinet were feeling."

CHAPTER TEN

Sybil was frustrated that she could not micromanage her attorneys in the law suit against the *National Enquirer*. She was occupied with some other matters viz. the repair of America's infrastructure, pending war with North Korea, and more than a dozen applications to the courts for states and regions to secede from her beloved union. And this morning–in the PDB–she learned from the ODNI of rumblings beginning to come from Iran.

DNI Admiral David P. Jacobsen, passed on intelligence from his spies buried deep within the household of Grand Ayatollah Ali Khamenei that the Supreme Leader told a meeting of the elite of the elite in the conference room in his residence that "Our brothers in North Korea are pulling the tiger's tail and may soon need our help. We gave them their atomic bomb, and now may be their chance to use it."

When he was asked how we could be so brotherly with a heathen anti-religious regime, he gave the expected answer: "The enemy of our enemy is our friend."

When asked for specifics, Khamenei told the surprised leadership, "We can place three nuclear missiles at the disposal of our new friends in a week. If they fire the first rounds, we will attack Great Satan's ships in Korean waters. They will not be expecting anything like that, and not from us. It will be like a new Pearl Harbor for them, and they are unprepared for a two-front war."

"How do you rate your source, Admiral," the president asked with all solemnity.

"A+, on a par with our source in the upper echelons of the DPRK. Both are true patriots, both believe the current regimes in their countries are tyrannical and need to be replaced, and neither will accept any money or promise of land or position from us. That is a clincher for me. We can control the ones who do it for money, but you cannot buy what these two assets can provide."

"I'll take it up with the NSA this morning," asserted the earnest president. "Khamenei is right, I don't think we *can* fight a two-front war; and, frankly, I have no intention of doing so. I am not going to sacrifice American lives for those two-bit countries with their madmen leadership. It continues to amaze me that those strutting martinets cannot see any error in their judgment or ways. They consider us to be a paper tiger. We are not."

Sybil had a luncheon meeting with the members of the NSA and the JCOS.

"I hate even to breathe what I am about to say, my loyal friends. But I am going to make a Top-Secret presidential order, we must prepare for a second war front against the

Islamic Republic of Iran. Before you is the outline for the reasons, and a preliminary outline for the measures we need to take. As time passes, I am certainly going to be amenable to suggestions. This is not undertaken lightly, as you can well imagine.

"In brief, I want you to accomplish two things in secret: First, send all but two of our carrier squadrons to the areas of Iran and North Korea loaded for bear. Second, since we apparently are going to face a two-front war despite our every misgiving, we need to activate the draft. Let's try and call up whatever number you deem necessary and get them started in training.

We can start with unemployed young men, the young black men in the ghettoes caught in the net of having a minor felony record and no hope for a decent job or life. Get the dust bowl farm boys and girls who are broke, out of work, and hungry. Look into homeless, but fit men and women. I am aware that many are there for no fault of their own, and this could be a dignified way out for them. Look for deeply indebted recent college grads who live with their parents, have no jobs, and have a pile of debt they can't pay. We can give them help and hope by removing their debt problems in exchange for honorable work.

"Any comments?"

"No, just a heavy sigh, Madam President. Will it never end? Will people never learn?"

"Good serious questions, General. I certainly have no answer for either of them. But, we still have to do what we have to do."

CJCS Gabler was more than usually pessimistic that day, "We're in the devil's ball game; we can't win; we can even break even; but we have to suit up for every game anyway."

Bryan Denbow, Clement Gioriani's attorney, and Roderick Michaelson, Sybil's private attorney began to have short facetime conversations twice a week. Denbow and his client were sure that the president and her attorney would wear down with the frustrating procrastination posed by their stubborn obfuscation.

"Look, Bryan," Roderick said, "I am earning billable hours; so, I don't really care how long you try to draw this out. Our position has not and will not change. If you just want to quit now, we have a deposition date fixed in concrete in Washington on December 23, 2022, and a court date at ten A.M. exactly a week later. You keep skirting the issue; I keep remembering it. The president asked for a deal she can't refuse. Give me a figure I can take back to her, at least. That will get the ball rolling at least."

"My client is difficult, I'll tell you frankly. I'll make an offer of $10 million. He'll scream, but he'll see the sense of it in a few days."

"That's the figure we had last week. I'm not going to take it to the president again. She'll think I've gone soft in the head. Sweeten the pot now, or I won't accept your calls anymore. See you in Washington in December, I guess."

"Don't stop talking. I will go way out on a limb and jack it up to $15 million, but I can't make promises for Gioriani. I'll give it a real try."

"I'm telling you, that is off by more than double. Give him the figure of $40 million; so, we can at least start to bargain. This is beginning to seem too much like negotiating in a souk."

At ten that morning after the PDB, Sybil had her monthly meeting with Speaker of the House Shirley Mair Zimbrowski who was acting in her role as head of the committee charged with repairing the infrastructure of the country.

"Good to see you again, Shirl," President Daniels said. "How is your son doing after his back surgery?"

"It was his third. A neurosurgery friend of the family told us not to have it done, that any back operation after two have been done and failed is doomed. He was right. My poor boy is in a lot of pain, and it won't go away. To make things worse, he has fallen into the quicksand hole where he needs good strong narcotics for pain; but he doesn't have cancer; so, no one dares to write him a prescription for fear of the government coming down on him and ruining his career. The real guidelines make a strong exception for treatment of people with irreparable structural injury to be able to get the pain meds, but doctors are too scared. They keep shifting him around for "second-opinions" or to another pain treatment clinic—anywhere to keep him out of their office. It's cruel, and it's a mess."

"And it's driven by an ill-educated press and readership. Once you say, 'opiate abuse', all minds shut down. I'm sorry he's caught in this quandary. It is indeed a mess."

"So, Madam President, let's get to work talking about a problem that is tough but solvable. We are very much in the same groove that President Eisenhower had to get to for his unprecedented transcontinental highway system be in place and functioning. He succeeded finally, and I am confident that we can also. Let's start with successes. It may not be fair to other cities or to any rural areas, but we had to scale things down and concentrate on the five boroughs of Greater New York City. We combined forces and treasuries with the state and city and started from the deepest down and are working our way skyward.

"We really could not start at the surface because we would have just had to dig it all up again. We sent the Sand Hogs down first. In case you are not familiar with the term, it has been around forever in New York. They are the tough bunch of guys who are now in the fourth or fifth generation at least. They are a society unto themselves. They are the urban miners and construction workers who work underground on a large variety of excavation projects in New York City and more recently in some other younger cities.

These projects include a combination of tunneling, mining, caisson excavation, road building, restoration of piping—some of which is well over a hundred years old. It is hard to exaggerate the value of these difficult to work with men and women; but nothing to do with subways, any size of water pipes, sewer lines, electric, or utility cable lines for anything you can imagine that makes our country work would be here without them.

"We have spent our first billion dollars, lost twenty good men, and have restored an estimated forty percent of the piping and utility lines underground. This repair should serve New Yorkers for a hundred years. We think we will be able to start rebuilding the municipal, state, and federal, buildings to bring them up to earthquake code in six months—cost another, maybe, six billion before we finish. Then we can finally start on the roads which are execrable. Figure a few more billions."

"A billion here, a billion there; after a while it adds up to real money," President Daniels laughed.

"The good news is that Chicago, Detroit, Minneapolis, Los Angeles, and San Francisco, are getting up some enthusiasm; and a lot of private donors and labor organizations are starting their own programs, all of which have the approval of our committee."

News of an important anniversary speech to be given by Kim Jong Un filtered in via encrypted messages in the middle of the night from the deep cover asset in his inner circle. The principle importance of the speech was that it was going to be given to a mixed audience of Iranian generals and admirals and North Korean elites. The asset reported as rumor but reasonably credible that the Iranian President, Hassan Rouhani, might be making a visit to the Hermit Country. It was news to most of the officials that Iran had a president and that the last prime minister held office until the revolution in 1979.

Two weeks later, the ever-useful asset was able to secrete out a recording of the speech and a verbatim transcript of it. It was chilling to think what he must have risked to do so. The speech was delivered at the Victorious War Museum [aka Victorious Fatherland Liberation War Museum]. Since early 2013, the captured American ship USS Pueblo (AGER-2) has been moored along the Pothong River in Pyongyang and used there as a museum ship.

"Countrymen and esteemed Persian guests, it is a great pleasure to see all of you on this auspicious occasion. I have decided to create a new holiday to link the two heroic occasions—the Blue House Raid, and the capture of the US Navy intelligence spy ship, the USS Pueblo and its eighty-three crew members. Our heroic navy put the Americans to shame that day—January 23, 1968 two days after thirty of our brave commandoes were murdered by the South Korean lackies and jackals. We made the great hegemonistic America grovel and plead and apologize to get its men back after a year. They threatened a nuclear attack, but we forced them to back down and to slink away. We kept the spy ship as a reminder to we citizens of the DPRK of our power, and to have our terrible enemies realize that we cannot be defeated.

"We pay tribute to our partners and friends of the Islamic Republic of Iran for their capture of the Great Satan's embassy and heroic detention of the spies who worked there. This created the now famous Iran hostage crisis–a diplomatic standoff between the United States buffoons and the heroic students of Iran. Fifty-two American diplomats and citizens were held hostage for 444 days from November 4, 1979, to January 20, 1981, giving all the world a great and daily laugh for a year and a half. How the mighty groveled and pled. How the country wept and wailed and gnashed their teeth and came begging hat in hand for the spies' release.

All praise to the Muslim Student Followers of the Imam's Line, who acted in support of the glorious Iranian Revolution, another lost war by the weak and posturing Americans. Those students took over the U.S. Embassy in Tehran and pranced the spies around like circus clowns. We in the DPRK danced in glee all those days.

"Now we are met to pledge our hearts and hands to more victories, and ones shortly to come, as we unite in our common goal. The Supreme Leader of Iran, and I, the Great and Dear Leader of all the north Koreans, shall soon make known our great plans. You may think the great victory of the 9/11 attack on New York City was glorious. But as those idiots in America would say, 'You ain't seen nothin' yet.'"

He laughed uproariously at his ever so clever jocular utterance, slapping his thighs. The North Koreans within hearing distance emulated the Highest Person in his every gesture, facial contortion, and tears of laughter, which continued for thirty-eight minutes until exhaustion finally forced the laughter to settle into titters and finally to grimacing smiles for the ubiquitous photographers.

The room was quiet. Sybil and her advisors were astonished by the news, even though they had had ample forewarning from previous experience with North Korea and its threats and antics. DNI Admiral David P. Jacobsen looked at his stunned audience and said,

"Let me give you a little background that will put things in perspective. The Brilliant Leader refers to the Blue House raid–also known in South Korea as the January 21 Incident—as one of the great victories celebrated in the Victorious Fatherland Liberation War Museum. Remember the charming fellow was preaching to his own choir and not to people who know better. The 'incident' was a raid launched by North Korean commandos called Unit 124 to assassinate the newly installed President of South Korea, Park Chung-hee. It was planned for two years with scrupulous attention to detail to kill Park in his residence at the Blue House, on January 21, 1968.

To make a long story short, thirty KPA [Korean People's Army] soldiers were killed, and one—a deserter—was captured intact. President Park was not harmed although quite a few South Koreans suffered the ultimate cost—hence, the victory.

"As a side note, Park was not exactly a charmer himself. He seized power in a 1961 violent coup d'état and ruled as a military strongman until his election and inauguration as the President of the Third Republic of South Korea in 1963.

"The other 'great victory', this one arguably, more or less a victory over us occurred on January 23, 1968. The USS Pueblo (AGER-2) is—note the tense–a Banner-class environmental research ship, attached to Navy intelligence as a spy ship and remains commissioned to this day. It was attacked and captured in what has come to be known as the 'Pueblo incident'. The place in history has some significance to us. The seizure of the ship and her eighty-three crew members took place less than a week after President Johnson's State of the Union address and week before the start of the Tet Offensive. We were not innocents: the Pueblo had intruded multiple times before. This was just the time when they got caught. The crew, minus the one who died in the attack were released at Panmunjom a year later—December 23, 1968. It would be the mastery of understatement to say that the Pueblo Incident still sticks in our craw."

"One more thing to add to our 'bad North Korea' list," said Sybil. "I am past beginning to lose my patience with that snot-nose Hermit Kingdom. One day they will cross every line and warrant a real comeuppance."

Her admirals and generals were learning to believe that when this president said something like that, she meant it. They liked that quality, and they respected her.

CHAPTER ELEVEN

Lieutenant General Mark A. Dietrich, chief of the NGA [National Geospatial Intelligence Agency] reported to the president and her intelligence officers during the morning PDB that the agency's satellites had collected thousands of pieces of photographic evidence that the KPA [Korean People's Army] were massing near the DMZ. The movements were done at night and with considerable stealth, but not secretly enough to escape being discovered by the NGA.

"Thank you, General. I will have a serious talk with my counterpart in South Korea. It is time they knew everything and began to prepare for the worst," Sybil said.

"Again," Gen. Dietrich said.

Sybil nodded.

Immediately after the PDB, she made encrypted calls to a number of agents she had dealt with during her long tenure as a CIA agent. These were men and women were special agents—specially selected, very specially trained serious experts from multiple military units and intelligence units who had–of necessity–been involved in wet work. No more than five people outside their very close knit, close mouthed, unit knew of its existence or the names of the people involved. Only Sybil and the unit leader, SA Howard, knew the particulars of the several missions they had undertaken. Even the previous president (Willets) was in the dark about the unit.

She was able to get through to Lincoln Howard, her trusted right hand during the Beelzebub Incident. Once she became president, Sybil had made Lincoln the chief of the President's Special Ops Group.

"Lincoln, it is nice to hear your voice again," she said by way of greeting.

"I like your voice, too, Madam President, but usually not the content," he rejoined.

"And, yes, my friend, it's one of those kind of calls. This line as secure as it gets, how about yours?"

"You, created it; so, I think we can say that it is as good as it gets. So, Madam President, it's your nickel, shoot."

President Daniels took an hour to explain the ongoing situations in North Korea and Iran and how the two rogue nations appeared to be conspiring. That brought her to the main reason for her call.

"So, Lincoln, you can see the pickle I'm in. If I start a war, half of the Americans will consider me to be a war-monger and a killer. If I wait until they commit an atrocity on our soil, and kill a lot of Americans, then, I am a fool and a coward for not knowing their intent and not doing enough about it when I did learn. Can't really win no matter what I choice I make about war; so, you see why I'm here."

"I guess I know the big why, but I'm waiting for the other shoe to drop; so, I'll know the 'what' of it that involves me and my President's Special Ops Group."

"I'll be exact," she said and tapped 'send' on her mobile to send an encrypted e-mail, 'eye-only' for Lincoln. "I just sent you a list of names, addresses, telephone numbers, and everything we know about certain important people in the two countries. There are no written instructions, but I'll give them to you in short hand: kill all of them, don't get caught, and don't get identified."

"Long list?"

"Quite. And an important one. We need to send a final message; the alternative is unthinkable."

"Secret, but unlimited budget?"

"As always. Report as often as possible, but don't leave yourself open to trouble just to report."

"Anything else?"

"Start ASAP. The cretins are getting ready to launch hellfire against Seoul. I need you to make them stop and think.

"Look, Lincoln, I know you and your people don't need a pep talk or a rehash of the danger and problems you face. But we both know that being a CIA spy might be the most exciting, challenging, and rewarding job in the world. It's all of that because I am tasking you with a set of objectives that would seem to be impossible—a list of assassinations of some of the most well-guarded people in the world and several of the most powerful in their respective countries. It's more than if I were asking you to steal the most closely-guarded secrets of our country's enemies or friends. You and your unit members are my friends, and I have the utmost respect for you. I will worry myself frantic until I know that you are back home and safe again.

"You guys are aware that you are part of a very, very small cadre that is capable and willing to undertake such a dangerous lifestyle. The job is lonely in that–unlike most other elite government agencies–you nearly always work alone. Even when in the company of your fellow operatives, you are forbidden to discuss anything with them unless they have a specific 'need to know'.

Your own small group makes it clear to all of you and each of you that–if one of your operations goes wrong– you will surely be on your own. It is possible that you will have no assistance and not even acknowledgement of your existence. Each of you carries a 'death pill'. That said, you know I will do all I can. You have my secret numbers and my emergency code. Use it only if you have no other choice."

Sybil knew when they left, and–in general–to where. Otherwise they were an entity unto themselves. Succeed or fail, no-one but her and the group members would ever know what happened. She silently wished them God's speed.

Atlanta was abuzz with excitement over what the verdict would be in the trial of the confederate secessionists. Sybil was kept informed of what was going on by a staffer or by taking a quick peak at the TV news. It was early morning in Atlanta, per the orders of Judge Jimmy Carter Hodson. He was a stickler about getting things done, done right, and on time. He was determined to end the trial phase that day and allow the jury to deliberate. Both the prosecution and the defense had rested their cases, and all that was left were the summations.

Attorney General Jacob Ryan Scottalia began his summation for the prosecution.

"Ladies and Gentlemen of the Jury, the United States, the State of Georgia, the City of Atlanta, and I personally, offer our thanks for the patience and attention you have shown during this tedious trial. I shall be brief in your interests and for the sake of clarity. You may ask the judge for anything that is unclear at this point and may be able to read from the transcripts of the trial thus far.

"As I stated in the opening statement, this is not really a complex trial. The issues are rather cut and dried. Was the late retired Sergeant Major Daniel Beauregard Jones murdered? If so, did the two-hundred and one defendants you have seen throughout the trial, led by self-appointed "Captain" Caleb Danby Macomb, commit the murder? Was the murder premeditated; that's what we lawyers call, 'with malice aforethought? Was the murder associated with exacerbating qualities. That means in this case, 'was the murder done as a hate crime? Was it especially cruel and heinous?

"You were able to see and here several witnesses speak to those questions: Rudolf Courtney, who was mere feet from the murderers and their victim; Rodger Coleman

Badger, Atlanta Municipal Police sergeant who was on duty keeping order along the parade route and who was also very close to the scene of the murder. He was the arresting officer; Agnes Brown, landlady of the deceased, who attested to the poor victim's good character and that he did not hate anyone, but he did exercise his constitutional right to speak his mind. He did so in a respectful manner, and they killed him for it."

"Objection! The learned prosecutor has not described evidence that Mr. Jones was killed because he was speaking his mind!"

"Overruled. But Mr. Scottalia, careful of making statements that remain for the jury to decide."

"Yes, Your Honor."

"Carry on."

"And there was Georgia State Trooper Lieutenant Thomas Calhoun, who testified as to the hate speech being shouted by the defendants and regarding their plans to kill the man standing before them making no offensive movements or speech. Last but certainly not least was the key defendant, Caleb Danby Macomb, himself. Mr. Macomb…"

"Objection! Captain Macomb has a right under rules of war to be accorded his rank!"

"Overruled. Make no mistake, Mr. Lee, the defendants are not POWs; no rank they put on themselves is recognized in any court in this land. I have been patient with your insertion of ideology in the place of evidence in this trial, and my patience is at an end. No further objections during this summation, Sir."

"*Mistah* Hodson," the defense attorney said to the presiding judge in a calculated slur, "Mah clients an' Ah do not recognize yah'all, this couat, this proceedin', or the legality of this heah countrah. They ah soldiers of a sovereign nation, the Confederate States of America. This is a kangaroo couat, Sah!"

"Officers of the court, remove Mr. Lee. He is in contempt of court. He may visualize the proceedings from a separate room via streaming television. When his time comes to deliver the defense summation, he may have the privilege of using a microphone, but not until then nor afterword. Mr. Lee, you are hereby sentenced to pay $5,000 and serve five days in the federal jail.

"You may continue, Mr. Scottalia."

Mr. Lee received a polite but prompt escort from the courtroom.

"Thank you, Your Honor," Scottalia said placing particular emphasis on the 'your honor', which did not go unnoticed. "As I was about to say before I was so rudely interrupted, my final witness of mention was Caleb Danby Macomb, himself. He confessed in this courtroom to all aspects of this heinous crime and had done so when questioned by US attorneys and prosecutors. It is no exaggeration to say that he expressed a puerile hatred of African-Americans and that he was proud of killing one in broad daylight with an audience of thousands. His justification was ludicrous—that he was a bona fide soldier at war with the United States.

"Ladies and Gentlemen of the Jury, this was premeditated heinous murder, a hate crime if any of us has ever known of one, and perpetrated by people who have stated that they wish to begin a war against our country; so, they can have a country which permits segregation, second-class citizenship for people of color, slavery, and extrajudicial lynching. I say to you, my fellow Americans, do your duty. Find these men guilty and come back with a penalty of execution. Much as I hate to say it, Mr. Macomb can only receive a sentence of life in prison without parole. Thank you."

Over the hastily set up television screen in the courtroom, defense attorney, Robert Alfred Lee, Esq. began to speak, more accurately to holler.

"Ah am an oppressed pusson who had been attemptin' to prevent a gross miscarriage of justice in this heah coatroom. No mattah what this socalled judge, who is nuthin' but a lacky for the Washington govahment, my clients and brothahs ah patriots seekin' justice frum an unjust coaht. They ah victims, POWs who have not been accorded theah God-given rahts. Membahs of the jury, do yoah duty. Ignoah alla the lies and fake news spewed heah. Send a message to the good what people of America that these men ah genuine patriots who rahtfully seek to secede from this heah union, to return to a time and place wheah what men had rahts and privileges. That is yoah duty!"

It was probably the shortest summation on record in the Atlanta Federal Courthouse—maybe in the country. It may have been the least appreciated ever as well, but that was up to the jury.

The jury received its instructions from Judge Hodges, who was obviously making an effort to keep emotion and emphasis out of his voice and frowns or eyerolling off his face.

It was noon, and the jury was excused for lunch and ordered to begin deliberations at two P.M.

Sybil N. Daniels, her cabinet members, law enforcement officers throughout the country, African-Americans, and secessionists all over, figuratively held their collective breaths waiting to see what the verdict, what sentence, if any, and what the aftermath would be.

South Florida based Special Agent of the FBI, Reginald O. Yang, contacted the headquarters office of the Chief Editor of the *National Enquirer Magazine*, Clement Gioriani. He met with the same obfuscating interference from the office secretary, then Mr. Gioriani's inner sanctum "senior executive assistant"–who looked like, walked like, and talked like, a secretary–that the civil lawyers had encountered. His organization was not particularly sympathetic to intentional procrastination. While it might not be entirely accurate that "the FBI always gets its man," it was rare indeed that special agents put up with avoidable impediments—which is how SA Yang characterized the efforts of the secretaries.

It was a particular thorn under Yang's saddle when he was told that Mr. Gioriani was "a very busy and very important man."

"Tell Gioriani that the FBI considers him a subject of interest in a matter of national security. He is to meet in my office in Miami at 1010 sharp tomorrow morning or become the subject of a federal warrant. If you want, you may tell him that I am a very busy man; and it does not bode well to evade me or to interfere with my ongoing federal criminal investigation. He is welcome to bring his attorney, if he wishes."

He did not smile when he said it, and he looked very serious.

It is remarkable how much communication can be enhanced when a sufficient stimulus is applied.

Less than thirty minutes after SA Yang exited the *National Enquirer* building in Boca Raton, Roderick Michaelson, President Daniels's private attorney, received a telephone call from that same building.

"This is Bryan Denbow, Mr. Gioriani's attorney, Mr. Michaelson," came the strained voice, which made Roderick smile a little.

"Hi, Bryan, why so formal? It's still Roderick here. What's up?"

"I think you know. You put them up to it."

"Do you want me to try and guess who and what you are hinting at? How many guesses do I get?"

"Don't play coy with me, Roderick. You know perfectly well."

"First guess, your rag has defied all good judgment and upped the ante by printing a new edition showing something very naughty being done by the president of the United States, and I should see it on the grocery store magazine shelves this weekend. Am I close?"

"Oh, give me a break. I am not in the mood for games. I thought we were negotiating seriously."

"I agree with the 'seriously', but I would call it 'slowly but seriously', like the Southern Democrats used to say about their foot dragging over the civil rights act issues, 'in all due diligence' to obscure their dilatory actions which–absent all the coded language–amounted to resistance to the implementation of federal government integration measures."

"I'll cut right to the chase. The fibbies came after us today, not an hour ago. I presume you know all about this, but I'll humor you. A Special Agent named Yang told our secretaries that my client would appear in the Miami Federal Court House tomorrow morning or become the subject of a federal warrant in a matter of national security. That's an egregious abuse of federal— read here, presidential, power—and hence illegal, my dear colleague."

"I've no idea what any of this is about. It's news to me. Do you know, Bryan?"

"If I knew, I probably wouldn't need to call you. Is this a threat to get President Daniels's will obeyed while trampling all over Mr. Gioriani's rights?"

"Not from my office or from any of my colleagues here or the president's office. I would be the first to know about anything like that."

"Look, Roderick, maybe I've been a bit hasty. But whatever is going on, you have Mr. Gioriani's attention. He wants to do business, and he authorizes me to negotiate in good faith if you, Anderton, Jukes, and the president, will reciprocate."

"Now?" asked Roderick.

"Better tomorrow after we have our little visit with SA Yang."

"I'll await your call, Bryan, enjoy the rest of your day."

At precisely 1615 GMT [Greenwich Mean Time] 2215—military time, EDT–a missile launch off the west coast of North Korea aimed at the center of international waters a few miles from the coast of Hokkaido, Japan hit an unintended target. As unlikely as a lightening strike on a lone individual, the missile impacted a large oil tanker causing an explosion recorded by satellites and every nondeaf person in Japan. US intelligence sources conveyed the information to the White House APNSA [Assistant to the President for National Security Affairs], who informed the president.

CHAPTER TWELVE

Japan's foreign minister cabled a strongly worded but polite message to his counterpart in the DPRK, Kim Young-nam, the head of state for foreign affairs. Minister Sora Kobyashi demanded full compensation for the massive fallout of metal pieces from the huge ship and for the clean-up of the largest oil spill in history. First estimates were ¥214,500,000,000.00 [$2.2 billion USD.] Investigations revealed that the ship destroyed was the Zeymarine Company ULCC [Ultra Large Cargo Carrier] TI class supertanker, the *Knock-Nevis* [aka, the *Seawise Giant*].

It was at the time the largest ship in the world; its length was equal to the height of the Kuala-Lumpur Petronas Towers ~ 380 meters. The TI Class of ships are the largest double-hulled supertankers in the world. The extreme costs of construction plus the fact that there are only three shipyards with the capacity to build TIs made them rare among vessels.

It was the pride of the Netherlands commercial fleet, valued conservatively at $91 million USD, and its cargo of three million gallons of oil at the price of crude that day being ~ $160 million USD [1 barrel = 42 gallons (0.136 tons) at $0.56 USD per gallon].

Speaking for the nation of Japan itself, above and beyond the obvious costs coming from the damages, Foreign Minister Kobyashi made it clear that this nonweather or nature caused incident—avoiding the word "accident"— would deprive Japan of its lucrative and important trade with its maritime border countries. Although Japan does not have any land bordering neighbors, there are a large number of maritime commercial partners: Taiwan [Republic of China], the Northern Mariana Islands [a US territory], the Philippines, Russia, South Korea, China, as well as North Korea.

More broadly, Japanese trade with North and South America, Europe, and the Middle-East, and the rest of Asia would be set back for many years. The cost would undoubtedly be in the billions, and the effort to regain trust and good will throughout the region would probably take decades—all of which would require compensation over those decades.

The foreign minister of the Netherlands send a similarly worded letter to that of the Japanese foreign minister, but it was not politely worded, and stated as a fact that the missile strike was not an accident; it was an attack—an act of war. He stated—almost matter-of-factly—that the value of the ship was over ninety million USD; its cargo one-hundred-sixty million USD, and only that low because crude was at an all time low.

Foreign Minister Curtiss Lathrope called full attention to and stressed the unimaginably impactful human loss—forty invaluable crewmen and four irreplaceable officers. His estimate—and he stressed that it was only preliminary—for compensation of the families of the crew would exceed sixty-million USD for actual expenses, not including future maintenance of the families, an estimated four hundred million USD. Minister Lathrope insisted that all those costs were very conservative.

The smell of cordite was in the air. Rumors of war and retaliation were flooding towards North Korea. But no reply came from The Wise Leader. He ignored the world and waited to see what the United States would do. The CIA's asset in the Kim household could only reveal that the Dear Leader found the missile engineer whose computer program caused it to land exactly as Chairman Kim had requested and unfortunately obliterated the largest ship in the world. The engineer was beheaded with a rusty bayonet. The sublieutenant who actually pushed the button was simply shot.

Sybil went into a huddle with the JCOS, the Secretaries of State and Defense, the heads of all seventeen intelligence services, and the APNSA.

"How do we respond?" she asked without revealing to anyone that she had already dispatched Lincoln Howard and his shadowy unit to North Korea. "I want every one of you to give me a two sentence reply to my question. Don't overthink it. Don't add a third sentence about the history of the United States and the Kim dynasty. As Joe Friday–the detective on the old series–*Dragnet* used to say as his catchword, 'Just the facts, Ma'am, just the facts,'"

No one took that as humor, least of all Sybil. This was another of her absolute decisions; that kind of decision making was becoming altogether too common with the Hermit Kingdom. One of these times—and probably not that far distant—Sybil Norcroft Daniels would have to have the last say.

Secretary of State Fiona Del Giordia spoke first, "Madam President, my team and I have studied the North Korean situation in depth. We are monitoring electronic communications and have learned that Chairman Kim is being pressed by some of his generals to make the DPRK more secure. That is code for putting pressure on Kim. Rumor has it that he is being backed up against a wall. That usually foreshadows an overt action for the benefit of his generals but not a move we have to be overly serious about. My suggestion is that we open very public talks with the DPRK, Japan, and the Netherlands… and including us, of course."

"Thank you, Madam Secretary. As the counter to that, let's have the secretary of defense have his say."

"Madam Secretary, my friends," said Secretary of Defense David Whitmer Smith, "I find myself in my usual place—polar opposite to the state department. For heaven's sake, how long are we going to let that little bully kick us around. The rest of the world is waking up to the fact that the only thing Kim and his generals understand is force and lots of it. We are building something of a coalition made up of the US and the countries impacted by the so-called 'accidental' missile strike on the largest ship in the world. They are: England, France, Germany, Norway, Sweden, Russia, Turkey, Israel, Saudi Arabia, UAE, Dubai, and Iraq. Take note that Iran, though impacted, is conspicuous by its absence."

Everyone nodded their understanding of the implications of that detail.

"The hermits backed down—way down—when we gave them a message via the satellite RedEye Laser. My vote is to do it again. We are the biggest threat to them, and if we exercise a small fraction of our power often enough, maybe they will get the message."

"Thank you, Mr. Secretary. Now, how about the DNI?"

DNI Admiral David P. Jacobsen stood for his delivery, "The aftermath fallout from the missile strike on the *Knock-Nevis* has been as great as if the strike was intentional. We are convinced that it was accidental, i.e. the ship happened to be in wrong place at the wrong time. The scuttle-butt in Pyongyang—coming from the Dear Leader—is that it was indeed intentional, a demonstration of the strength of the DPRK and its missile forces to be able to stand up to us and the rest of the hostile world. Privately Kim murdered the men responsible for the strike. Mixed signals are altogether common from the Hermit Kingdom, always have been. Our suggestion is that we have our special ops forces send a signal or two or three in the form of covert assassinations."

"Thank you, Admiral, I'll take your suggestion under advisement. I'll ponder for a bit and then send a communique by two. Keep your eyes and ears open for anything new coming from the peninsula. Enjoy your lunch," the president said by way of adjourning the meeting.

Her decision had already been made, and the executors of that decision were en route.

Mary Carpentier poked her head into the Oval Office. "Time turn on the TV, Madam President. It is about to hit the fan in Atlanta."

Four network screens lit up in the Oval as the jurors marched into the courtroom in Atlanta. The room fell silent, only interrupted by the bailiff's order of "All rise".

Judge Hodson looked at the jury forewoman, Dorothea Wilson.

"Have you reached a decision, Madam Foreperson?"

"We have," she said and handed a folded paper to the bailiff who delivered it to the judge.

Judge looked at the decision for a long minute, then gave it back to the bailiff for delivery to the jury forewoman.

"Please read the verdict, Madam Foreperson."

Dorothea adjusted her glasses, then read: "As to count one, 'murder in the first degree', guilty; as to count two, 'capital murder with aggravating circumstances', guilty; as to count three, 'felony incitement to riot', guilty; as to count four, 'conspiracy to commit murder and to incite a riot', guilty. The decision of the jury was unanimous and applies to all 201 defendants."

The courtroom was divided into two equal sides—ordinary citizens, mostly African-American on the right, and members of the CSA organization, all dressed in Confederate uniforms on the left. When the forewoman finished her reading of the jury's decision, pandemonium broke loose; and two dozen separate fist fights started.

The chaos was expected, and a small army of bailiffs, city and county law enforcement officers, and half a dozen special agents of the FBI moved into the room in force. From the time Judge Hodson's gavel hit the desk until the court room was empty, fourteen combatants were quickly arrested, read their Miranda rights, and whisked away to jail, less than six minutes had elapsed. Law enforcement and military units were barely able to contain the street violence outside the courthouse. Atlanta had a full-blown riot on her hands.

Snitches confirmed that the riot had been planned by the CSA for weeks. It was the secessionists main tactic to gain recognition—the moment to capture enough attention in the citizens to get the measure to the Supreme Court the quickest way possible. There was a strong sense of collusion among the other secessionist groups and the CSA because peaceful marches in a dozen or more cities and towns introduced the public to the secessionist movement at large, and because—in each of those cities— more motions for secession were introduced.

If the staff at the *Enquirer* believed that the attention on Atlanta by the president and her people would materially distract them from the defamation suit, they were sadly mistaken. President Daniels had given all necessary orders for riot control around the country to allow life to go on and the secession issues to proceed through the courts in an orderly manner. She was very much ready to follow her attorneys as they made and responded to offers and counter offers today.

Roderigo Michaelson called Bryan Denbow instead of the reverse this time. He was ready to make a serious offer.

"Good morning, Roderigo. Glad to hear from you this fine day. Is Washington in any danger from the southern riots?"

"None that I am aware of, Bryan. Anything there in Florida?"

"Oh, yeah. Most reasonable sized towns and cities are having parades and the like. The big population centers are mired into serious riots."

"Sorry to hear it. Now to business. The president and her three attorneys have agreed on an offer. First, you pay $32 Million, 2nd, there is no nondisclosure clause: the *Enquirer* can make up its own story. The president and I plan at least a short book to explain the other point of view. 3rd there is no limitation, foreign or domestic, on any kind of information being made public," Roderigo said.

"Money's probably okay, but Gioriani is in it to prevent the government from destroying the *Enquirer* by using the president's not inconsiderable resources."

"Take it back to your client, Bryan. Try to get a signature. I assure you that you and your client will not like our next steps."

"Is that a threat?"

"No, Bryan, just a heads-up. It's your turn to call me next. Until then, keep safe."

Sybil had three more meetings on her agenda for the day: national rebuilding and repair, plans for announcement that the Senate would complete its advice and consent duties and approve Senator Franklin H. Tatum of California as the new vice-president, and the first meeting with her campaign committee for the upcoming presidential election—her second.

Gen. Gabler and his entire committee met with President Daniels on the east lawn of the White House for a celebratory picnic. It was the second anniversary of the beginning of the rebuilding of the country. Gabler announced that the projects were more than half done. Most of the eastern cities had finished their projects and were spanning out to share what they had learned and to help in the actual work.

Speaker Zimbrowski was presented with a commemoration plaque for being the overall head and first CEO of the New America Volunteer Force. President Daniels was honored for her foresight in including Volunteers for American Revival as part of her reinstituting the military draft as a preparation for possible war with either North Korea or Iran...or both.

For all the grumbling and even lawsuits, the draft was becoming a considerable success. Ghetto boys with minor records were given jobs and dignity. Rural boys and girls got a chance to see the wider world provided in cities. All of them were introduced to diversity, different ways of believing, thinking, and acting. There was renewal of enthusiasm for America that even Sybil's critics could not deny.

Sybil's campaign manager, Sawyer Nielson, was full of good news. Her approval rate was climbing steadily. That day polls indicated that she had a 54% approval rating and compared to the two other candidates from the Democrats and Republicans she was ten points higher than the Democrat and fourteen above the Republican in election preference.

Sybil met Frank Tatum in the Oval Office for a brief last-minute opportunity to reassure him, and to get a final chance to look at him and into him before making the big announcement.

"You look great, Frank. You are the right choice, and I will work to make your job fulfilling for you as well. I want you to have real work—it's good for the soul. I want you to take on the thankless job of revitalizing the inner cities and their people, and no less of a project—make it your work for the next four years to create some sort of harmonious relationship between the good citizens of the ghettoes and law enforcement. We have talked about the creation of committees and assessing real needs, finding employment for young men with minor records to keep them out of gangs. Think you are up to that, Frank?"

"I was afraid I would just become one of those footnote veeps and be bored to death. This sounds like just my kind of thing. I'll be a good boy and give you the credit; just let have the authority to get things done."

"I will not take credit for work you do. Be responsible and keep me in the loop is about all I will ask."

"Madam President, it will be a pleasure to serve you."

"With me…" she said, and they both smiled.

Sybil formally introduced Senator Tatum to the speaker and the majority leader, and they all discussed the long-awaited announcement. It was an uplifting day for the government and for the people. Things were looking up in most areas of the country, and the people were responding with a sense of hope.

Sybil had concerns; her most sincere hope was that this positive time could last.

CHAPTER THIRTEEN

The FBI agency secretary met *National Enquirer* senior editor, Gioriani, his attorney, Bryan Denbow, and his paralegal, Dotty Truman, in the outer office and offered them a seat and a small bottle of water while they waited. They were nervous about the meeting; so, they had arrived fifteen minutes early.

"Special Agent Yang will see you in a few minutes. Make yourselves comfortable."

They waited fifteen minutes, and Clement Gioriani, senior editor of one of the largest newspapers in the world did not sit and wait for anyone. They sat and waited for him.

"What a lot of gall this guy has," he said to Dotty, "who does he think he is?"

It was a rhetorical question, but she answered anyway, "He is John Law."

"And what am I, chicken liver?"

Dottie never answered such unwinning questions.

The agency secretary finally came back.

"Follow me, please," she said.

They walked down a long hallway until they came to a door on the left marked only with a small sign, "Room SA 13."

"And now we have to sit in the unlucky room," Gioriani griped.

"Wait here," the secretary said.

The room was fairly small but well appointed. The furniture was attractive stained oak with brass button finishes on the leather. There was a green and cream color hand knotted carpet. It was designed with large squares which—for all its richness—was a little unsettling. Dotty, especially did not like it. The desk was cluttered with documents and folders lying askew. There were no softening features, not family photos, no sports trophies, and no pictures of SA Yang shaking hands with the president or other dignitary. The only window looked out onto the asphalt parking lot.

SA Yang entered and took his seat behind his chair behind the desk without shaking any hands or offering a pleasant greeting.

"We're busy people. Let's get right to it.

"Mr. Gioriani, do you know a man by the name of Terry Gimbaldi?"

The senior editor thought about the question for a moment, obviously debating whether to answer.

The pause was too long, SA Yang answered for Gioriani, "We're wasting time. You and I both know that you do. I'll ask a similar question, "What is the nature of your business with him?"

Gioriani and Denbow whispered to one another.

Yang raised an eyebrow.

Finally, Gioriani answered, "Okay, I know the man, so what?"

"Is your relationship personal or business?"

"Both, and again, I want to know, so what?" His expression reflected both defiance and a tinge of curiosity.

"He is a drug lord with a long rap sheet across state lines and international borders. We are investigating his associates in the United States, especially Florida. You are one of them."

"Me?!, I barely know the guy."

"Come, come, Mr. Gioriani. I have some photographs that may interest you."

Yang laid out twelve large prints from an array in his hand. Three of them were photographs of the sitting president of the United States in compromising scenes and positions. The rest were of clandestine meetings between Gioriani and a large thug who Gioriani instantly recognized as the man he knew as Terry Gimbaldi.

"Recognize these, Sir? Remember, Mr. Gioriani, you, Mr. Denbow, and you, Ms. Truman, lying to a federal officer is a felony. We have already had a long and revealing discussion with the man who photo-shopped these photos so that our nice president's head attached to persons involved in debauchery. Mind your answer, Mr. Gioriani."

"Yeah, okay, I know the creep. He has ties with the Russian criminals. He did the pix."

"And you paid him for the work?"

"Yeah."

"Did he make the arrangements?"

"Yeah, after I paid him a bunch a moolah."

"Do you have other business dealings with the Russian mafia?"

"I guess you could say so…maybe."

Denbow leaned over to whisper in Gioriani's ear again.

"Yeah, we do some work together."

"Would it be fair to say that you are engaged in an ongoing criminal conspiracy with the *rossiyskaya mafiya*, or *Bratva*, a known OPG?"

"What's a OPG?"

"That's an internationally accepted acronym for Organized *Prestupnaya* Group—or OCG, substituting Criminal for us English speakers. So, now that we understand each other, start talking. The more you talk, the more I learn; the more I learn; the easier it goes for you. Am I getting through?"

Gioriani dropped the arrogant insolence.

"Yeah. What do you want, Special Agent?"

"Somebody to pay my mortgage, but I'll settle for everything—and I mean everything you know about that gang. Let's start with the photos of the president."

"Not without a guarantee of immunity," Bryan Denbow interjected.

"Let's hear what you have to give me, then, I'll decide. I'm honest, and I will grant you some form of immunity if you are entirely forthright, and if the information is helpful to the government's case against the OPG."

The two *National Enquirer* executives gave each other serious looks.

"Okay, you got me. Let's see, you wanted to talk about the president's pix. They woulda cost a bundle, but the Russkies said they had other, more important uses; and they gave us a bargain."

For the first time in the meeting, Dotty Truman spoke up. "I want immunity, too, the whole Megillah. I know plenty of stuff to make it worth your while. But, I'll keep mum unless you let me off free and put me in WITSEC."

"Guaranteed, Ms. Truman, with the same big 'if'. You *will* get your say."

She pointedly stood up and moved six chairs away from Gioriani and Denbow.

FBI Director Horace Eyring informed the president and her attorneys about the details of SA Yang's telling conversation with the *National Enquirer* people. The result was a very different discussion among the president's attorneys and Bryan Denbow the following week.

"Roderick, my client has decided to settle. He wants to get this monkey off his back."

"So, Bryan, is this going to be for real, or is it time for the president to show her cards?"

"Claws, you mean," Bryan said.

"Call it what you want; but professional gamblers call it the 'upper hand'. Let's hear your offer. And, Bryan, this had better be good, because the president is very tired of this. She does not suffer fools lightly, and Clement Gioriani has become an annoying fool of late."

"How does $35 million and a complete NDA sound?"

"Two days ago, I would have thought about it for a minute. You are perfectly well aware that things changed drastically then. Try again, once more. I repeat, *once* more."

"Oh, Roderick, let's not belabor the point. Tell me what you want. You have beaten us."

"$40 million, with your client donating twenty mill of that to American reconstruction, and the president will donate the rest to the same organization (s). There will be no NDA. She is going to write or ghost a book, and that's that. Say nasty things if you want, but you better keep them true enough to be on the side of the angels. Let's just say that President Daniel's is now a regular reader of your muck rag. And, finally, we talked earlier about how a retraction and an apology are to be presented. All of this happens in a week or less, or we start again from scratch. The next time 'scratch' will be $60 million."

"Okay, okay, okay. It's extortion, but you get your way. The only thing we require is that the president makes no mention of Gioriani's dealings with the FBI."

"I'm feeling generous. I'll get President Daniels to agree to that proviso. Our dealings are done, Mr. Denbow."

All eyes and ears in the Atlanta Federal District Court turned Judge Hodson. It was verdict day. Reporters held their pens poised over their note pads. The families of the defendants had their fingers crossed. The defendants had lost their bravado and sat in expressionless stony silence.

The judge sat at his bench resting his chin on his hands, lost in thought. The courtroom became silent. People barely breathed.

He directed his attention to the defendants, "The jury of your peers has unanimously found every one of you 201 men guilty of murder in the first degree, capital murder with aggravating circumstances, felony incitement to riot', conspiracy to commit murder and to incite a riot, guilty. The decision of the jury was unanimous and applies to all defendants. The jury recommended implementation of the death penalty for all but one–Caleb Danby Macomb–and for you, Mr. Macomb, life in prison without the possibility of parole because of a plea bargain with the US Attorney's office.

I am responsible to see that justice is done; so, I hereby vacate that plea bargain. You, Mr. Caleb Danby Macomb, and every defendant, are sentenced to death for these capital offenses. The mode and date of execution will be determined by the corrections department of the United States penal system. May God have mercy on your souls. I know there will be controversy as to whether a judge has the right under the law to change a plea bargain. I submit that there is no law against it, and justice can only be served if justice and its penalties are equal. Court is adjourned."

Judge Jimmy Carter Hodson banged his gavel, and pandemonium broke out in the courtroom and spread into the streets.

-The End-

www.ingramcontent.com/pod-product-compliance
Lightning Source LLC
Chambersburg PA
CBHW060751180626
46818CB00002B/539